The Haunting of Shadow Hill House

By

Caroline Clark

Copyright © 2017 Caroline Clark

All Rights Reserved

Caroline Clark

License Notes

This Book is licensed for personal enjoyment only. It may not be resold or given away to others. If you wish to share this book, please purchase an additional copy. If you are reading this book and it was not purchased then, you should purchase your own copy. Your continued respect for author's rights is appreciated.

This story is a work of fiction any resemblance to people is purely coincidence. All places, names, events, businesses, etc. are used in a fictional manner. All characters are from the imagination of the author.

TABLE OF CONTENTS

Prologue 1
Chapter One 11
Chapter Two 27
Chapter Three 43
Chapter Four 61
Chapter Five 75
Chapter Six 87
Chapter Seven 101
Chapter Eight 111
Chapter Nine 119
Chapter Ten 129
Chapter Eleven 141
Chapter Twelve 159
Chapter Thirteen 167
Chapter Fourteen 173
Chapter Fifteen 179
Chapter Sixteen 189
Chapter Seventeen 195
Chapter Eighteen 207
Chapter Nineteen 215
Chapter Twenty 225
Chapter Twenty-One 239
Chapter Twenty-Two 251
Chapter Twenty-Three 259
Chapter Twenty-Four 267
Chapter Twenty-Five 275
Chapter Twenty-Six 283
Chapter Twenty-Seven.. 297
Epilogue 313
Preview: The Haunting of Brynlee House 317
Preview: The Haunting of Seafield House 329
About the Author 335
Copyright 337

Prologue

May 24th 1690
Shadow Hill House,
Crick Howell
Wales,
United Kingdom.

11.02 pm.

    Closing her eyes tightly, Victoria clutched Mr. Good Bear to her chest and tried to shut out the noise. Mr. Good Bear was her favorite toy and the smell and feel of him always gave her strength. He was a brave bear and was hardly ever afraid of the dark. Yet it was so dark that she knew even Mr. Good Bear would be a little scared. Outside, the storm raged against the window threatening to come in and wash her away. She did not know where it would take her but she knew it would not be good.

The sound of rain on the glass was like a million tiny fingers all trying to get in, all trying to get to her. Try as she might she could not shut out the sound and yet part of her wanted it to get louder. She wanted it to drown out the noise of shouting and crying that had woken her. Why was this happening again? It didn't make sense.

Before she could decide on an answer a scream rang out through the night and Victoria backed further under the bed. This was her safe place, this was where she came whenever the shouting got too much or the monsters too close. Usually she could put her fingers in her ears, rest her head on Mr. Good Bear and shut out the noise but tonight she was so frightened. Maybe it was the storm. Maybe it was the flashes of lightning that lit up the room and yet left so many shadows. Victoria hated the dark, hated the shadows. Things hid in the dark and lived in the gloom of the shadows. Things she didn't want to think about but they were creepy, crawly and had hands that reached out and grasped you when you couldn't see them. The monsters came in the dark and the monsters scared her almost as much as Daddy. Yet, when she was under the bed she was safe. It was a bubble of protection that no monster could cross. Mummy had told her she didn't need it but Victoria knew she was wrong. Under here she was safe and the monsters could slink and slide around the room. Their greedy hands clasping for her but they would never find her if she kept still and quiet. It was hard to keep quiet. With every noise she let out a little gasp and her breath was coming so fast she was sure the monsters would be drawn to her.

"Safe," she whispered. "Safe in my bubble." Tears escaped her eyes and slipped down her face to land on Mr. Good Bear. "Keep quiet, must keep quiet," she sobbed and tried to still the beating of her heart. Tried to still the blood rushing through her ears but it was no use. As much as she wanted to hide she also wanted to hear. She wanted to go to Mummy, wanted to be safe in her arms. To be told the monster wasn't here and yet Mummy was crying and she sounded almost as afraid as Victoria was. That was one of the things that Victoria could never understand. Mummies weren't supposed to be afraid. They were strong and they chased away the monsters. If Mummy was afraid then maybe she had lied. Mummy always said the monsters weren't real but if Mummy was afraid then that shadow in the corner wasn't just a shadow.

As lightning flashed Victoria got a glimpse into the corner. It was so quick and so full of shadow that she couldn't really see and yet she did. Big red eyes were peering back at her. Huge teeth glinted and glistened with saliva and then were gone, swallowed by the darkness just as the monster would soon swallow her. Victoria knew she should always hide when the shouting started but tonight she couldn't. Tonight, Mummy was afraid and so was she. It would be better if they were together, they could comfort each other and Mummy would keep her safe. Maybe she could bring Mummy back and they could hide under the bed with Mr. Good Bear.

"Would you help me hide my mummy?" she asked and automatically she tilted the bear to nod his approval. It made her feel better. She was not alone.

Another scream rang out through the night. This one was tortured and spoke of pain and fear.

Victoria knew she had to go, that she must get past the monster and yet suddenly she could not move. The room was so dark and yet the darkness was full of darker and these were the bits that scared her. She could only see the bottom of the room, as she peeked out from under the blankets that she had arranged so they almost touched the floor, and yet she was sure she could see things moving.

Another scream rang out through the night and Victoria let out a sob. Only now she found she could move. Clutching tightly to Mr. Good Bear she shuffled out from under the bed and ran to the door. Her hand was slick with sweat and it slipped on the handle. Her breath was coming in short shallow gasps and she could feel something behind her. Was it the monster? Desperately, she tried to hold the handle, tried to turn it but her hand kept slipping. Now she could feel the breath of the monster on her neck. It was cold and it smelt bad. Before she realized, her bladder loosened and hot urine was running down her legs. There was no time for shame, it did not even register over her terror and at last the door handle opened. Pulling it towards her she slipped around the door and raced down the corridor towards the shouting.

Surely Mummy and Daddy wouldn't shout if she was there. She knew Mummy had told her to ignore them. That it didn't matter and that no matter what, she must never to come when Daddy was shouting. Only they would understand because of the monster!

The corridor was dark and long and curled around the house. There was a banister to her right and doors opened on her left. She thought there were six but was not sure as she could not count. Hers was the furthest room from Mummy's and sometimes she hated that. At night she would lie awake and wonder if they would hear her if the monster came. What if she was asleep and the monster came? Would she be eaten before she could wake?

It was hard to run in the dark and her bare feet slapped on the wooden floor so hard it almost hurt. As she raced onward it felt as if she were falling and she wheeled her arms and saw a glimmer of light ahead, a ray of hope. That was Mummy and Daddy's room; that was a sanctuary from the monster. Would she make it in time?

Fear gave her legs speed and she raced towards that light, towards safety.

It seemed to take forever to run the length of the hallway and every step of the way the monster got closer. Victoria could feel it behind her, could hear it behind her and she ran faster and faster, blind with panic. Her legs were flapping, her arms were flapping. Mr. Good Bear was clutched tightly in her right hand; he seemed to be willing her along. She raced as fast as her legs would carry her and yet the light seemed so far away. Would she make it? Would the monster eat her just moments away from safety? At first, she thought the monster was making a noise, it was a little huck, huck, huck. Soon, she realized that it was her and she tried to stop the crying. Everyone knew you had to be quiet when the monster was there and so she ran faster, ignoring the shouts and screams that she was running towards.

Mr. Good Bear was urging her on. Willing her to safety. In her mind she could hear him telling her to run faster, just a little faster. Though he could not stop the monster he could help her with that and he did. Soon they would be safe with Mummy for she could see the door ahead. Tonight, it was open, which was unusual and for a moment she faltered. Then the monster roared and the house seemed to quake beneath it. Crying out in alarm she raced towards the open door.

As she reached the door, lightning lit up the room and the sight before her was almost as bad as the monster.

Mummy was lying on the floor in front of the bed. Blood and bruises covered her face and there was terror in her eyes. Victoria clutched Mr. Good Bear, holding him to her chest she sucked on his ear. Normally this would calm her but not tonight. Tears were streaming down her face and she wanted to go to Mummy but she could not move because the monster had gotten around her and was blocking her way. It was bigger than she remembered and twice as scary. Once more, the monster roared and Victoria wanted to cover her ears and dive beneath Mummy's bed but she could not get to it. She tried to point, tried to talk, to tell Mummy to get under the bed but no words came out and Mummy just sat there. Didn't she realize it was safe under the bed?

Lightning flooded the room and the monster turned to Victoria and suddenly it all made sense.

The monster was Daddy and he was going to eat her.

Light glinted off a blade in his right hand and then the room was plunged into darkness once more. A flickering lamp in the corner barely chased away the gloom. Victoria could hear moving but she could not see anything. Standing as still as she could she tried to make herself small. That was another way to beat the monster. If you were so small, quiet, and so still, it wouldn't see you. Maybe it would go right on past you so why was Mummy crying, didn't she remember all the tricks she had told Victoria to beat the monster?

Victoria stood in the dark, trying to be small and insignificant as she listened to her mummy sobbing.

"Victoria baby, go back to your room," she sobbed out the words. "Everything's okay, baby, just go back to your room and Mummy will come and see you soon."

At first the words were just noises and Victoria couldn't make them out, but then she gradually understood them and she wanted to turn and run but her legs would not move.

The daddy monster growled again and almost immediately the house was filled with light. Victoria let out a scream as she saw the monster stalking closer to Mummy. A long claw in its right hand was raised and just before the darkness fell it slashed down. Victoria screamed and felt something warm and wet splash across her face and arms. It covered Mr. Good Bear and that made her want to cry.

Monster juice all over her bear that should never happen.

As her eyes became accustomed to the dark she saw the monster turn towards her. She knew she must run, must get back under the bed and yet her legs would not move. The monster approached her and roared again, only this time it was not as loud and she knew it was words, only she could not understand them. Shaking, she clutched Mr. Good Bear to her chest and tried to stop the tears. Maybe she could talk to the monster, if it was talking to her, and yet she could not understand what it was saying.

"Have you wet yourself again?" The monster roared. "You are such a pathetic child." The monster roared again and this time they were no longer words it was just a stream of vehement anger and filth.

As Victoria tried to sink into the floor the monster grabbed her and she was yanked from her feet. She knew it was the end, that she was going to be eaten and she let go of Mr. Good Bear, hoping that at least he would escape. In the foyer below, the old grandfather clock chimed the 15 minutes. It was 11.15 pm.

Chapter One

April 3rd, 2017.
Shadow Hill House,
Crick Howell
Wales,
United Kingdom.

3.02 pm.

Jenny Evans felt her tummy tighten as they turned off the small lane and onto the long sweeping driveway. Trees lined each side and sunlight dappled across the bonnet of the blue Cavalier as they accelerated up the hill.

The atmosphere in the car was thick and heavy and she feared things could only get worse. Mason was angry with her, angry at himself, and instead of looking at this move as a new opportunity he had become more petulant than Abby who sat behind them playing on her tablet.

Jenny could understand Abby being

upset. At 7-years-old this was a big move. She had left behind all her friends, her school, her home. Everything that was familiar had gone and Jenny understood why her daughter was hurt. Turning, she smiled at Abby. They had the same brown eyes and the same long black hair. As slick as a raven's wings Mason once told her and she remembered how it made her feel uneasy. Abby had her dad's lips which were fuller than Jenny's but that was where the similarity ended. Jenny gave her daughter a smile and was rewarded with a grin. It lifted her sadness and filled her with hope. They were a family and they would get through this.

Of course, they had to; this move had left them in serious debt and with nothing to fall back on. Jenny felt a moment of doubt. What if she failed, what if her idea, her dream was just that? What had she done to her family?

As they climbed the hill to approach the house the sun went behind a cloud. Would it rain while they were moving in? Jenny hoped not and she sneaked a glance at Mason. Beneath a mop of short and always unruly brown hair, his jaw was clenched tight and his hands gripped the steering wheel so hard that his knuckles showed white. Steel blue eyes stared out the windscreen and she heard him tut when he saw the house sign.

It was hung at an angle and looked old

and battered. Shadow Hill House was barely readable beneath the peeling paint. Weren't the contractors supposed to have changed it? Jenny noted that it would need to be changed. She wanted her guests to have a good impression and this was the first thing they would see.

Then she thought of the contractors. How they had promised what would be done and then how George Draper had rung her just two weeks ago and told her they could not finish the job. That something had happened and they would return a percentage of her money. She had been unable to get an answer from him as to what the problem was and wondered if one of the men had been involved in an accident. George had assured her that enough of the work was done for them to move in and so Jenny had been relieved. It reduced the amount of overdraft they needed to get this place up and running.

The car continued to climb up the hill before turning a corner and the gothic mansion came into view. The sun came from behind the clouds and seemed to spotlight the house. It was just as beautiful as Jenny expected and she drew in a breath. A large white house stood before them surrounded by green. There was a circular turret on each side of the front door topped with the cutest pointed roof. For a moment, she just stared and took in the beauty of the place. They were at the crest of the hill.

The house surrounded by its own gardens and then countryside. She could see a woodland to one side and fields spread out below. It really was a most idyllic setting and instantly Jenny saw the lawn filled with artists. All painting the wonderful scenery or even the house, their house.

She turned to her right as Mason slowed the car and pulled it up on the circular driveway. His mouth was open and there was a look of wonder on his face. Before she could feel happy, it was gone, replaced with a look of worry and then even that was gone, replaced with his now familiar scowl.

Once more her stomach tensed. This was supposed to be a new start for all of them and yet without his help, without his support, it would be so much harder.

"Wow!" Abby said from the back seat. "It's so big and like a castle. Can I have the room in the turret? Please, please, please, I will be like a princess."

Jenny let the tension go and got out of the car. There was a slight breeze but it was warm and invigorating, the clouds had passed over for now. She took a moment to look around. This was the perfect place to paint and the perfect place to raise a family. No crime, no pollution, and plenty of fresh air and places to walk.

Abby was already out and running towards the house.

"You'll need the key, silly," Jenny called, and then felt a moment of panic as Abby opened the front door and disappeared inside. "It's unlocked," she said, but Mason was taking no notice. He was unloading cases from the boot and could not hear her. Feeling uneasy, Jenny left him to it and walked up to the house.

The driveway was old tarmac and weeds were showing in places. It was not bad but still gave an impression of neglect, and she realized it would need to be cleared. Maybe they could spray?

As she neared the house she could see the paint was a little faded. Again, it was not too bad but did it give the right impression? It didn't matter. There was no more money. They would be living on next to nothing as it was until the first guests arrived and she received some income. How long was that? Just over six weeks. Luckily, some had already paid and that would have to tide them over for the foreseeable future.

The door was open as Jenny approached but just before she got to it, it slammed shut with a resounding crash. A shock raced down her arms and her pulse rocketed. "Abby," she called and reached out to the handle. At first it would not turn. It felt as if someone was holding it on the other side and Jenny felt her panic rise. It fluttered in her chest like a trapped bird as she imagined her little girl hurt. The door had been open. Was someone here? Had someone got Abby?

Just as she had the thought, the handle turned and she rushed in. The sight before her took her breath away. The hallway was almost as big as their old flat. It was decorated in a deep, dark, red. Sangria red according to the contractors and it was so open and bright. The floor was rich mahogany wood with a deep red and blue carpet that covered most of the floor and swept up the huge staircase that curled around the back of the hallway. Hallway, how could she call this a hallway? It was huge and magnificent and she imagined it full of guests. Of excited artists all chattering and getting to know each other. It was a dream come true.

Four dark paneled doors lead from the room and a magnificent chandelier hung from the ceiling. It was so high up that Jenny felt her neck crick as she took in the view.

She had almost forgotten Abby until she heard a shriek of delight from upstairs. Quickly she raced for the sound, her mother's instincts unable to hear the joy in the squeal and her heart pounded in panic.

"Abby," she called as she stopped at the top. The hallway was long and there were so many doors.

"In here Mum, bagsy my room."

Jenny followed the sound down the corridor to the furthest room. She stepped in and was overwhelmed with the beauty of the décor. The walls were decorated in wallpaper with small pink flowers. The carpet was a deep pink and the bed spread complimented the walls. There was a sheer pink canopy over the bed and the same sheer pink material surrounded the windows. Abby was stood looking out of the turret window, a huge grin on her face. Then she turned and jumped onto the bed.

"This is perfect," she said. "Thanks, Mum."

"I guess this is your room," Jenny said, pleased that something had gone to plan and yet, she distinctly remembered telling the contractors that the rooms must be decorated in a neutral tone. Until they arrived they could not know which room Abby would take and the builders had taken a huge risk decorating this one for a child. What if Abby had wanted another room? Shaking her head she supposed it didn't matter. Abby was happy and they would work around that.

Jenny wanted to explore the house, she wanted to look around and was so excited to do so.

"The movers are here," Mason shouted from below. Jenny could tell that he was still angry.

"Why don't you stay here and enjoy your room while we get everything moved in." Jenny said to Abby.

Abby just nodded. She was lying on her bed, tablet in hand and didn't seem too worried about anything. Breathing a sigh of relief, Jenny made her way back to the stairs. Now if only it was that easy to make Mason happy. She smiled at the thought of him sitting on a princess's bed.

By the time she got downstairs Mason had already got everything organized and the men were busily unloading boxes.

"The essentials are in the kitchen. Why don't you get the kettle on and I'll see to this," Mason said.

Jenny gave him a smile and for a moment he just stared. So she widened her smile and stuck out her tongue. This always worked, this always made him smile. For a long moment nothing happened and she felt her spirits sag. Was he so angry with her, so hurt that he would not make an effort? Before she could answer a smile broke his face and suddenly they were laughing. She wanted to say something, to tell him it would be all right and yet she knew she mustn't. So she stuck her tongue out even further and then turned and raced to the kitchen.

The kitchen was a medley of old and new. The dark wooden cabinets looked as if they had been there forever. As if they belonged in the house and yet the work surfaces were a black marble that gleamed at her. There were three windows looking out at the garden. On one of them a blind was fitted. On the next one the blind had been fitted at one end but was draping down at the other and the third window the blind was waiting on the floor. This must be one of the jobs that the contractors didn't finish. If this was all it wouldn't matter. Mason could soon fix up these blinds and it would give him something to do.

The floor was made of black slate and at one end of the room was a small breakfast table. The kettle was next to an old ceramic sink. Quickly, she filled it and turned it on. While the kettle boiled she began to unpack boxes. There was so much cupboard room, so much room everywhere and she could not help but smile. As she unpacked she remembered first seeing the house. It had been three weeks before Mason was made redundant and even then she was drawn to it. She had been flipping through an old magazine when she saw the property for sale and instantly she wanted it.

Yet, even if it hadn't already sold there was just no way they could hardly afford the house they were in. To buy a property of this size and to move away from Mason's and her job... It was nothing but a dream. Only she had had this dream for years. An artist's retreat she used to call it. A place where she could teach art to people who really wanted to learn. Her job at the college was teaching art but most of her students were just there for an easy ride. They were not interested, they were not passionate, and the work did not fulfill her. In her retreat, she would teach people who wanted to learn. She would mix with like-minded individuals who loved color and perspective. People who wanted to learn, who wanted to see behind what they painted and wanted to develop their art to the next level.

Once he was made redundant, the idea just kept coming back to her. It was a new start, a new beginning. Mason had a small redundancy pot and so one day she rang up about the house. Amazingly, it was still for sale and they were prepared to lower the price so she spoke to Mason. At first he was angry, but eventually she talked him around to at least listening. Before he would even consider the move and purchasing such an expensive property he had insisted that she ran adverts. That she tested the water to see if she could get clients. He had been amazed at the response. Jenny would only teach five people at a time and she was charging them enough to make that viable. The first advert she placed was oversubscribed by 200%. The bookings came in so fast that she was already booked up for the following year. In the end, she raised her prices even more because there were so many people that she could not cope with the demand.

Once she had the clients it was just a matter of buying the house, having it renovated and now here they were. Four months later, deeply in debt, it was all down to her to make a go of this.

It had taken just two hours for all their worldly goods to be moved into the house and for the men to leave. Now she knew she had to face Mason and yet she did not know what to say. What could she say to bring him out of his mood? They were here now, they had to make the best of it. Fried chicken was cooking in the oven and so she had some time. Stepping out into the hallway she could see a pile of boxes but no Mason. So she started to explore.

From the front door the first room on the left was the ballroom. It sounded grand and as she opened the door she was assaulted with a musty smell. It was almost as if something had died in there and she had to bite back the urge to vomit. This was just what they needed. Only she would not let it get her down, whatever happened they would cope with it and they would make the best of this. Ignoring the smell she walked in. It was a beautiful room, not as big as she expected but big enough to get 5 artists with easels and plenty of room for all of them to work.

The floor was dark wood paneling and the walls were paneled at the bottom and once more painted in a deep, dark red on top. There were five windows and the corner of the room was round and obviously part of the turret. It was beautiful and the light should have been perfect and yet the room seemed dark and a little dismal. Jenny felt uncomfortable there and yet she could not put a finger on why. So she left the room and carried on exploring. Next was the dining room. It was a good size and she could see it filled with her guests, could almost hear them talking. It was also wood with a blue and red carpet that matched the hall and dark mushroom-colored walls. As she left the dining room a shadow crossed over her and she felt herself shiver. Suddenly, she felt alone and so empty. It was as if no one was here, as if Mason had taken Abby and left but that idea was just silly. As she turned, for just a moment, she saw a figure hanging from the ceiling and then it was gone. A gasp left her and her hand flew to her chest. What had she just seen? It didn't make sense. Then she laughed, it must just be a shadow, maybe the sun passing behind a cloud or even her own shadow. How could she be so silly? And yet in her mind she saw the figure of a girl, a young girl hanging and it was hard to shake it from her mind.

BANG, BANG, BANG.

Abby jumped at the sound behind her and for a moment she could not work out what it was. Then she let out a laugh. It was simply someone knocking at the door. Maybe it was a neighbor coming to welcome them. Though she didn't know where they'd come from for the closest neighbors were several miles away. With a hand trying to steady her pounding heart she walked across to the door and pulled it open. An old lady stood there, she must have been in her 60s, maybe even early 70s. Gray hair topped a wizened face and yet the eyes were hard as slate.

"Leave, you have to leave this place," the woman said as soon as the door was open.

"We only just moved in," Jenny said, not sure what the woman meant. "We just bought the place. My name is Jenny, Jenny Evans, and I'm pleased to meet you." Jenny held out her hand.

"I've warned you," the woman said. "Shadow Hill is cursed, you have to leave."

Jenny knew she was staring, that her mouth was open and she could not formulate the words to reply. The woman was trying to peek around her, trying to look into the house and Jenny stepped across to block her view.

"You have no right to tell us this," Jenny managed. "We bought this house, we intend to run a business from it. If you can't be pleased for us just go."

"Oh, my Lord," the woman said. "You have children?"

Jenny didn't know what to do and she answered without thinking. "Just a daughter, Abby."

"Abby will die unless you leave," the woman said.

Jenny felt as if she had been hit. To hear someone say that about her daughter was worse than being assaulted.

"Mason, Mason, get down here please, quickly," Jenny shouted. At least Mason could chase this woman off. Would make her go. She could hear him moving on the floor above. Only, when she turned back to the door the woman was gone. Jenny rushed out of the house and yet she could not see her. There was no one on the drive, no one on the lawn and no car in sight. How had the woman got here? Where had she come from and why was she threatening her daughter?

Suddenly, Mason was at her side and she just wanted to be in his arms, just wanted him to hold her and for things to be back as they had been. Had she made a big mistake buying Shadow Hill House?

"What is it?" he asked.

"There was a woman, an old woman, she threatened Abby."

Mason ran outside and looked around, but there was no one there.

"There's no one here," he said. "What do you mean a woman threatened Abby?"

Jenny did her best to explain but she could see he did not believe her. Where could the woman have gone? It didn't make sense, the ground was open, there was nowhere for her to hide and yet she was gone. Jenny didn't know what to think and had to bite back tears. She knew this was going to be difficult. That there was hard work and hard times ahead but she never expected her beautiful Abby to be in danger. The thought that a mad woman could be out there, after her daughter, chilled her to the bone.

Caroline Clark

Chapter Two

Mason turned around and went back inside almost dismissing her and her fear.

"I've had our clothes and things put into the main bedroom," he said. "Do you want to unpack while I work on the study?"

Jenny nodded and he led her up the stairs and turned right towards the bedroom. They walked all the way along the corridor further and further away from Abby's room. With each step Jenny felt more nervous. Why were they taking a room so far away from their daughter? Mason showed her into the room. It was beautiful. Dark red walls and a dark red carpet. The bed was a four-poster made of hardwood and the drapes were a deep crimson. Jenny shivered as she walked through the door, it was cold in here.

"We're a long way from Abby," she said.

"I don't see that it matters," Mason

snapped before he turned and left the room.

Jenny felt as if he was shutting her out and yet she knew there was nothing she could do. This had happened before and it was always best if she left him to it. Since being made redundant he had changed and she knew she needed to give him time. To let him discover his purpose once more. Hopefully, this move would help, they could work together and build something great.

So she looked around the room. Tt was obviously the master bedroom just as the one she had been in before was obviously a child's bedroom. Why did she feel nervous being so far away from Abby? Maybe it was just the strange woman, maybe it was the new house. She didn't know but before she decided to unpack she was going to check the other rooms. To see if they could move closer.

She went back out into the corridor and started looking at the other rooms. The one next to them was smaller and plainly decorated, the only furniture was a crib. That seemed really strange. They hadn't asked for a crib or for anything for a baby. It didn't matter, the room was not suitable for Abby. She spent the next 20 minutes looking into all the other rooms. They were all designed for guests and quite obviously so. They were plainly decorated, smaller, with a small wardrobe, desk, and an ensuite shower and toilet. Some of them were not finished. A few had doors that needed hanging and one needed painting. The tin was still on the floor along with dust sheets. The lid was off and a dried up paintbrush had stuck to the carpet. Jenny let out a sigh, still it would give Mason something to do. She took a last look around. There was no way that Mason would move into one of these rooms of that she was sure. So she walked the full length of the corridor back down to Abby's room and knocked on the door.

"Hey, Abby, how are you doing?"

"I'm fine, Mum. I love my new room." Abby barely glanced up from her tablet.

"Do you mind that you're a long way away from us?"

Abby raised her head and gave her a look that was entirely too old. It said, *be serious!*

"No, I'm a big girl now and fine all alone."

Jenny wanted to laugh but she knew that would not be a good idea so she nodded and walked back to their own room. It really was a long way and it worried her thinking about it. Yet, why should it? What could happen?

With no answer to her question she started to unpack. Only she felt uneasy in the main bedroom, as if the atmosphere was heavy and weighing her down. As she packed away their clothes and toiletries she pushed the feeling aside. Her little girl was growing up, becoming more independent, that was why she was feeling sad. Then there was Mason. He had disappeared and was keeping himself scarce. It was almost as if he was sulking. She knew he would be setting up the morning room as an office. They had talked about it before. As a chartered accountant he was hoping to get a few clients. How the world had changed; a few years ago, he was in demand and now he had been thrown away like yesterday's news. She understood how he felt and how much it hurt him to not be able to support his family. Maybe he would get work here. Maybe he would soon have a thriving business.

Jenny closed her eyes and wished it so. Taking a moment, she relished in the move and let her dreams and hopes seep back in. Let the belief that she could do this take over. It felt good. She imagined walking amongst the artists, first in the ballroom, and then outside on the hill. It was such a perfect position, there would be so much light and views in every direction. The peace and quiet were perfect for deep concentration. She saw herself looking after her clients, encouraging here, and assisting there and a smile turned up her lips. They could do this. All she had to do was keep her head.

Opening her eyes she felt a shadow cross over her and she watched it flit over the wall. It was just the clouds, but even that was a delight. In their flat, surrounded by other taller tower blocks they rarely received direct sunlight. This would be so great for Abby, the countryside and all this fresh air. Turning, she saw a patch on the wall at the side of the bed. For a moment she thought it was the shadow but that couldn't be right. Then she gasped, it looked like blood. It looked slick and wet. Slowly she approached the wall and the stain grew as she watched. How could this be?

Jenny looked around, it was not the sun. Of that she was sure. Turning back the blemish filled her vision and seemed to pull her eyes to it. Tentatively she reached out her hand. Stopping just millimeters from the wall. For some reason she didn't want to touch it and yet she felt drawn to it. With her breath held she touched the wall and let out a chuckle. It wasn't wet, cold maybe, but not wet. Maybe it was a damp patch? Maybe this was another thing the contractors hadn't finished.

Feeling the sudden urge for some company she turned and left the room.

Downstairs, she saw the morning room door shut. It felt like a snub and she hovered with her hand above the handle. Maybe she should just walk in. Ignore his behavior and shame him out of it. At the last moment she changed her mind. She had to give Mason time. Had to let him come out of this on his own.

The smell of burning drew her to the kitchen. She checked her watch. There were still 10 minutes before the chicken should be ready and yet the smell was getting worse. Rushing in she saw smoke coming out of the oven and she turned it off and pulled open the door. The room was filled with thick black smoke.

Coughing, she opened the back door, grabbed a towel and pulled the pan from the oven. It seared into her skin as she rushed out the door and dropped the hot pan onto the ground. Blackened chicken rolled onto the paving and she rubbed her scalded fingers. They were starting to blister and yet that shouldn't have happened. How many times had she picked up a pan with nothing more than a towel? It was too many to count and she had never burnt herself before!

The chicken was ruined, her eyes were running, her throat sore and her fingers stung. Quickly, she made it back to the kitchen and turned on the cold tap. It spluttered and splashed her with ice cold water. A curse hovered on the tip of her tongue but she bit it back and reduced the pressure. Gradually the water stopped spluttering but when it started to run it was brown and she let out a cry of disgust.

"What is it?" Mason's voice was urgent and close.

Jenny looked around and was surprised to see him there.

"Tea's ruined," she said and showed him her fingers. They were red and already blistering.

Mason rushed forwards and took her hand pushing it straight under the cold stream of water. Jenny tried to stop him and she felt a shudder of revulsion pass over her.

"You have to get this under the water," Mason said as he held her hand firm.

The cold did ease the pain. "But... but... the water," Jenny started but as she looked the water was running clear and smooth. The spluttering had gone and so had the awful color, she relaxed and let him hold her hand under the stream until the pain eased. Mason took it out and gently dried her fingers. The blisters had popped and he looked through a few boxes until he found the first aid kit. Gently, he applied some cream and then bandaged up her fingers.

"Did you pick the pan up with your bare

hands?" Mason asked.

Jenny knew she hadn't and she looked at the thick towel lying on the floor. "I used that," she said.

Mason raised an eyebrow.

"Well, maybe it slipped. I was panicking because of the smell. Way to make the house smell like home."

Mason laughed. "I don't know, I think your cooking's improving."

Jenny was filled with relief that he was teasing her. It was a glimpse of the old Mason. However, she was not letting him get away with it so she picked up the towel and flicked him on the backside with it before squealing and running out of the room as he grabbed a towel in retaliation.

Abby found them a few minutes later. Racing around the patio flicking each other with towels and laughing fit to burst.

"I'm hungry," Abby said, looking at them as if they were children. The look of disgust on her face had them both laughing again. Mason scooped Abby into his arms and carried her into the house.

"Well, Princess," he said. "How about I

cook us up a bit of cheese on toast?"

"Yes, Daddy, yummy, yum, yum."

"We're in Wales now," Jenny said. "It's Welsh Rarebit, not just plain old cheese on toast."

"I don't want to eat rabbit," Abby said. "Specially not Thumper."

"OK then, just plain old cheese on toast for us all," Jenny said as she found out the bread and cheese.

Soon they were all tucking into platefuls of cheese on toast and they seemed like a family again. Mason poured them both a glass of red wine and Jenny found she was starting to relax. This was what she wanted, a new start, and a new future.

"What do you think of the house?" she asked.

"There's a lot of work that needs doing. Those cowboy contractors seem to have just dropped tools and run."

"I know, there's even a paintbrush stuck to the carpet in one of the upstairs rooms." Jenny waited for him to get annoyed, waited for the tension to mount, only this time it didn't.

"We've got six weeks," Mason said. "Tomorrow, let's have a good look around and make a list of everything that needs doing. I'm pretty sure I can handle it all as long as we prioritize."

"I wonder why they left?" Jenny asked.

"Beats me," Mason said, "but enough of the house for tonight, why don't we all snuggle up on the sofa and watch Lady and the Tramp."

"Me, me, me," Abby said as she leaped out of the chair and started running from the kitchen. Suddenly, she ground to a halt and turned to look at them her face all serious. "Where is the telly?" she asked.

Jenny felt suddenly tired. It had been a long day traveling and then unpacking and she knew the telly would be in one of the boxes but the thought of hunting through and finding it as well as the DVDs was beyond her. Only Mason had a smile on his face.

"I knew my princess would want to relax," he said. "Come with me." With that he left the table and, grabbing Abby's hand, he led her into the hallway and then to the room to their left. Jenny had not looked at this one earlier and was pleased when she walked in. It was a large living room and Mason had set it up with their furniture. The black leather sofa and chairs looked a little out of place in the ornate beige room and the telly that looked huge in their flat looked minute here. Still, everything was ready for them. Mason laid back on the sofa and Abby curled up in his arms. Jenny picked up his feet and sat with them on her lap. This was their routine when Abby was up. Later, once she was in bed, Jenny would take her place and they would curl up together.

As they watched the film Jenny began to feel herself drifting and by the time it was over Abby was asleep and she was so tired she decided to call it a night.

"Do you think we should have an early night?" Jenny asked.

"I was going to put an advert on the Chamber of Commerce website," Mason said. "I'll carry the munchkin up and you bring your glass of wine."

That sounded like a good idea so she followed him out and into the hallway. Once again she saw a shadow skit across the floor of the hall and felt her skin prickle with adrenaline.

"Did you see..." she started to say, only it was already gone and already she did not believe it had been there. It must be fatigue... and yet she had seen a figure, a shape hanging from the banister.

"See what?" Mason asked as he carried Abby effortlessly up the stairs.

"Nothing, it was just a shadow."

When they got to the room there was an old fashioned teddy bear lying on the bed. Jenny picked it up.

"Did you get her this?" she asked. It looked grubby and the fur was stiff in places. Jenny decided that she would wash it tomorrow.

Mason shook his head as he laid Abby down.

"No, maybe it was in the house."

"Maybe," Jenny said.

Abby never woke and Jenny changed her into her night clothes and tucked her into bed. Mason had already gone back to his office and Jenny stood and watched Abby for several minutes. She seemed so comfortable, so relaxed, and yet Jenny worried. What if she woke in the night and couldn't find them? Then she laughed. Abby never woke. She had always slept so well they had been really lucky.

At last she left the room leaving the door ajar before walking back the long length of the corridor to their own room.

For a moment she saw a shape in the corridor and she started to call out thinking it was Mason. Only it was gone before her mouth could open and she dismissed it and walked on rubbing her hand along the banister rail.

It seemed to turn colder as soon as she entered their room and for a moment she felt a pinprick of panic. What was wrong with her? This was her plan, her dream and here she was worrying because Abby's room was so far away. Maybe it was the thought of the guests. Strangers sleeping closer to her daughter than she was. What should she do?

For now she knew there was nothing but maybe in time she could move Abby to one of the closer suites and have it redecorated, maybe.

Jenny undressed and climbed into the bed. It was cold and made her shiver. She picked up an art book she had left on the bedside table and, sipping at her wine, she began to read.

It was over an hour later when she found herself drifting and wondered where Mason was. Should she go find him or just go to sleep?

In the end she got up and, grabbing a robe, she started to leave the room. As she passed the stain she was drawn to it. Once more it looked wet, slick, and it made her think of blood. There was a central tinge and then splashes radiated from it. As she looked it reminded her of one of the forensic shows on telly. It reminded her of cast off blood splatter and she found a shiver run down her spine. When she looked at that blemish she felt... threatened. It was as if she was in danger and yet that was stupid. It was just shoddy work from the contractors. Just something that needed another coat of paint. Yet, what could cause that stain to appear through the paintwork? Maybe it was just damp. If not what could it be?

"You know."

"What?" Jenny could have sworn she heard a voice, telling her she knew what it was, and yet there was no one here. Was it just her mind playing tricks? It must be. She was tired and angry at the substandard work and she was looking for answers.

Turning, she left the room and went all the way back down the corridor to the stairs. The lights were off downstairs and the house looked dark and shrouded in shadow. For a moment she wanted to go back to bed. Only not to their room, for a moment she was drawn to Abby's room, it felt safe.

What was wrong with her? Being spooked by a strange house was just plain silly.

So she flicked on the light and walked down the stairs and into the morning room. Mason was sat at his desk just staring into space.

"Are you all right?" she asked.

For a moment he didn't move and then he turned towards her and his eyes were dark and menacing. Then it was as if he woke and he smiled weakly.

"I must have drifted off."

"Come on, let's go to bed," she said and offered him her hand.

Mason took it and they walked towards the stairs. As Mason turned off the lower level lights a piercing scream echoed through the night. They both jumped. Jenny was gripping onto Mason's hand so tightly she could feel her nails digging into his skin.

"What was that?" she asked.

Mason was tense, his breath held and the sound sliced through the night once more. A mournful scream that raised the hairs on her neck.

Mason started to laugh.

"It's not funny," Jenny said.

"Yes, it is," Mason said. "That's a peacock."

"A what?"

"You know, a big fancy bird with an amazing tail, a peacock. I've heard them before."

"But who would have a peacock out here?" Jenny asked.

"Maybe it lives in those woods behind us." Mason shrugged his shoulders.

"Are you sure?" Jenny asked, and even though he nodded she did not feel any better. As they walked up to their room she was on constant alert. Waiting for the noise to repeat but nothing happened and the silence was almost as bad as the scream of the peacock.

When they climbed into bed Mason fell almost instantly asleep and yet Jenny could not rest. She lay awake for hours listening for any noise. The house creaked and groaned, ticked and tapped but there was nothing else. Nothing too sinister and yet nothing seemed familiar and every nerve in her body was on high alert and she felt filled with dread. As if unseen eyes were watching her, as if someone was waiting.

Chapter Three

The morning came too soon and Jenny felt fatigued as she struggled out of bed and yet she could not rest. Something was nagging at her, something she needed to do, so with a heavy sigh she decided she may as well get up. Mason was snoring loudly so she snuck into the bathroom and washed and dressed as quietly as she could. Sun shone through the curtains, it looked like a wonderful day, and yet she could not shake the feeling of disquiet. Maybe she just needed tea; it was a standing joke in the family that she never functioned until she had had her first 3 cups. So she left the bedroom and went down to the kitchen. All was quiet and peaceful. Normally, on a morning like this she would make herself a quick drink and then set up her easel. Then she would paint, oblivious to the world until Abby or Mason came to disturb her. Only this morning she didn't feel inspired. Maybe she was just tired, maybe the move was too much and she needed a day or 2 to unwind... and yet with such wonderful views... she stared out the kitchen window at the woodland just beyond the garden. It was green and lush and full of so many different shades and colors that it should have inspired her but still she felt nothing. The sound of the kettle pulled her out of her daze.

Once the tea was made she set the table for breakfast and was surprised to find it was gone nine. Upstairs she could hear sounds of movement. It seemed that Mason was up and she hoped he was in a good mood. Hoped he was optimistic. Quickly, she made him a coffee and took it upstairs.

The sound of whispers was coming from Abby's room and Jenny found herself smiling. She loved to hear her chattering away to herself and she stood on the landing for a few moments just listening. Then she turned and took the coffee down to their room.

"Morning," she said as she walked in but was surprised to find Mason still in bed.

He rolled over all bleary eyed and peered out from under the sheets.

"What time is it?" he asked.

"Just gone 9.15. I thought you were up, I thought I heard you moving."

Mason sat up and took the coffee, rubbing at his eyes.

"No, not me, it must be Abby."

Jenny nodded, she could have sworn the sound came from this end of the house. The thought disturbed her, what if somebody was here? It was a big place, what if someone had snuck in and was hiding from them? Then she almost laughed. It was an old house but new to them. A different house was bound to make noises she didn't recognize. Leaving Mason to his coffee she stepped back into the hallway and looked to her right. At the end of the corridor was a small, almost hidden stairwell to the loft. For some reason her eyes were drawn up to it. So far they had not ventured up there but she remembered from the plans of the house that it was all boarded out. She had thought about making it into a store room and decided that before the week was out that she would make her way up there. The sound of whispers came again and she swung around trying to find the source. It sounded like it was coming from the loft but it had to be Abby and so she turned and went to see her.

As she approached the room she could hear the whispering and she felt relief. It must just be the acoustics of the place playing tricks on her. The whispers must have been Abby all along.

Abby was having a conversation with someone and Jenny couldn't quite hear about what. For a moment her heart clenched and her breath caught in her throat as she imagined an intruder in the room with her little girl. What was wrong with her? All children talked to themselves or their toys, and that was all this was. As she knocked on the door the whispering stopped and she stifled a giggle.

As she walked into the room her breath caught once again. Only this time it was because of how beautiful her little girl was. In her pink pajamas, with her hair all tousled and her eyes barely open, she really did look like a princess in the pink canopied bed.

"How did you sleep?"

"It was lovely, Mummy. I love my new room and teddy kept me company."

Jenny shuddered as Abby pulled the dirty teddy from under the covers.

"That's really nice but I think Teddy needs a bath. Why don't I do that while you get dressed and then we can have breakfast?"

As she reached for the bear Abby snatched it away. This was not like her, not like her at all.

"No, no, Mr. Good Bear doesn't need a bath?" Abby said as she hugged him to her chest.

The dirty bear held by her daughter really disturbed Jenny but she didn't know why. She had never been one of those parents who stopped children getting dirty. That was just a part of life and yet there was something about this bear that she didn't like. Maybe this attitude was just a reaction to the move but it didn't matter. If she was keeping that thing then it was having a wash.

"Well, you know what happens when you say you don't want a bath."

For a second Abby looked cross and then a smile broke out on her face.

"He won't come clean," she said. "Victoria told me so."

With this she handed the bear over and got out of bed.

"Can I play outside after breakfast?"

"I don't see why not," Jenny said, but she felt a little disturbed. Maybe it would be hard to let her girl out of her sight but this was the country and it was safe to do so. However, old habits die hard and maybe it would be harder than she thought to adapt.

***

They were soon tucking into a breakfast of bacon and eggs. In the sink, the teddy bear was soaking in a bowl of hot water. Abby kept glancing at him and Jenny knew she really wanted to have the bear but she was not backing down. First he needed a thorough soak, then she would scrub the stain from his chest, then after he had been dried Abby could have him back.

"There are a few jobs I want to get done today," Mason said. "These blinds need fixing up, doors need hanging, and there's a lot of painting to do. Looks like the damn contractors skipped out on most things. But the thing that's bothering me the most is the stains on the carpets. I really think we need to do something about them."

"What stains?" Jenny asked as she sipped at her tea.

Mason's eyes widened and for a moment she thought that they would argue again. Only then he relaxed and took a bite of his bacon.

"The master bedroom has a big stain and there is another one in the hallway."

"The one on the wall?" Jenny asked.

"I think that's just a few splashes of paint... unless it's a damp patch," Mason said. "I'll paint over it and if it goes, fine... if not, it's gonna take a bit more stopping. We will need some specialist paint and a builder to check the roof. I assume that is where it is coming from. I was talking about the stain on the carpet."

What stain on the carpet? "I never noticed," Jenny said, and she felt strangely disturbed. Mason was not the sort to take a lot of notice. If he had seen it she should have seen it. Then she shook her head, what did it matter? He was taking an interest and that was exactly what she wanted.

"Do you think it will scrub off?" she asked.

"I think we'll need a carpet cleaner. While I'm doing a few jobs why don't you nip into the local town and hire one?"

Jenny nodded. It would be nice to get into the town, to pick up a few more bits of shopping and to see the lie of the land.

After breakfast, she tidied up the pots and loaded them into the dishwasher before having one last scrub at the teddy bear. Then she rushed the dripping bear outside and hung it on the line. It would be dry for later, she just hoped the stain had gone.

As she hung the bear on the line she saw a car pull up into the drive. It was an aging Ford and it pulled around to park. A man got out from the car and looked over. He was young, perhaps just 25, and wearing a black shirt and trousers. At his neck was the distinctive white flash of a collar. They were getting a visit from the local priest. For a moment Jenny felt a little annoyed. It had been a long time since she had gone to church and she did not feel the need for his interference. Still, she wiped her hands on her jeans and offered a smile.

"Good morning," he said in a soft voice that sounded more like London than Wales. "My name is Luke Jones and I'm your local priest."

He held out a hand and Jenny shook it.

"Good morning," she said.

"I just wanted to come along and welcome you to the area, and to tell you that I am here if you need anything."

Jenny smiled... now came the sales pitch. "That's very kind," she managed.

"I'm new to the area as well," he said. "I only started here a month ago."

Jenny noticed that he was suddenly nervous and she felt rude. "Can I offer you a drink, Father?" she asked. "Tea or coffee?"

"That would be very kind," he said.

Jenny pointed the way to the kitchen. Mason and Abby were still sat there and she introduced the priest. She could see Mason raise his eyebrows. He seemed annoyed and yet she was only being neighborly. While she made the drinks there was a stony silence at the table. The young priest tried to make conversation but it was not going well. At last Jenny put cups of coffee before them and sat down. Maybe she could make a little conversation.

"Thank you," Luke said. "I haven't had a chance for a coffee this morning so hopefully this will wake me up a little."

"I'm always the same before my tea," Jenny said. "Do you live locally?"

"Just on the outskirts of Crick Howell, you will see the church as you drive into town. I find it very quiet and a little strange after London."

"Me too," Jenny said.

"Victoria doesn't like you," Abby said without any warning. "She doesn't want you here."

Jenny watched the young priest's face pale and turned her eyes on Abby.

"That is rude, young lady. Now

apologize and go to your room."

"It's all right," Luke smiled and seemed to suddenly be at ease. "Who is Victoria?"

"She lives here," Abby said before Jenny could stop her.

"She's my daughter's imaginary friend," Jenny said. "Now, young lady, apologize and off you go."

"I'm sorry, but Victoria's not," Abby said before stepping from the table and running out of the room."

"Oh, I am so sorry," Jenny said.

Luke laughed. "At least she's honest. I wish other people would be like that."

"Oh, well, I really am sorry. How did you come to move here?"

"It was the first post that came open after I left the seminary. How about you? This is a beautiful house but from your accents I feel like we were probably neighbors before?"

Jenny explained a little bit about the artists retreat and she felt Mason bristle as she mentioned the redundancy.

"I'm sure a good accountant will be in high demand around here. I will ask around for you if you like?"

"I would appreciate that," Luke said.

"Well, that's settled then. I really must be going but feel free to pop in and see me at any time. It was lovely to meet you." With that Luke stood up and was gone.

***

Before she left for town, Jenny looked at the carpet in the hallway and sure enough, there was a big stain directly under the banister rail. It pulled her eyes to it and yet made her feel a little sick. As she stepped back it looked to be in a shape but she couldn't make it out. Letting out a big sigh she walked up the stairs to grab her bag and a jacket. Once she was above the stain she looked down over the banister. It was just to see if it showed from up here and it did. Now she could see the shape. It was an angel. An angel of blood stained the carpet.

Quickly, she pushed that thought aside and strolled down to the master bedroom. The stain on the carpet was just where Mason said it would be. This one was not so artistic and was more like a puddle. It looked wet and sticky and yet as she reached down it was simply rough. Her eyes glanced to the wall and the splashes were still there but were not as bad as the carpet. How could she have missed it? It didn't make sense but then maybe she wasn't looking for problems. Maybe she had been looking at this house with rose colored glasses. Seeing only what she wanted to see. Anyway, it didn't matter, the stain was there and it needed removing.

"Abby," she called. "Do you want to come into town with me? We can pick up a magazine and one of those chocolate eggs you like."

Abby was outside playing and she didn't answer. Jenny picked up the car keys and left the house. Abby was sat on the lawn holding that horrible bear. Jenny wanted to grab it from her, after all, it would be soaking, and yet she knew that was the wrong thing to do. For once she was going to bribe Abby.

"I'm going to town, if you come along we can get a magazine, maybe stop for a hot chocolate and ice cream and get some of those chocolate eggs. You know, the ones you really like with the surprise inside." Jenny couldn't believe that Abby was hardly responding. She hadn't even turned her head away from the bear and was bouncing it on her knee and talking to it.

"Mr. Good Bear doesn't want to go," Abby said.

"Well, Mr. Good Bear should be drying on the line."

"He's already dry, Mummy, and he's ready to play."

Jenny couldn't help herself, she walked over and reached down and squeezed the bear. Abby was right, it was dry. It didn't make sense and yet Jenny felt too tired to try and work it out.

"So, are you staying here?"

"Yes, me and Mr. Good Bear are going to play, and maybe Victoria will come soon."

"Who is Victoria?"

"She's my friend," Abby said.

Jenny just laughed, not sure if Victoria was a real friend, or one of her old friends from Facebook, or someone local that she had met. Maybe she should check her account again later. Just to be sure she wasn't talking to anyone she shouldn't be.

"Okay, I will tell Daddy you're staying. You stay close to the house. You understand?"

Abby nodded but didn't look up from her game with the bear.

***

The trip to town took about 20 minutes and Jenny was quite surprised at how remote the house was. She had passed only one house on the drive into town and yet, wasn't that what she wanted? Somewhere remote, somewhere beautiful and isolated. Somewhere where she could put all her energies into painting and so could her guests. It was a beautiful drive, everywhere was green. Idyllic fields dotted with fluffy white sheep and copses of delightful woodland. Suddenly, she was feeling happy again. As she entered the small town of Crick Howell she saw the church. It was a beautiful stone building with magnificent stained glass windows that seemed to wink in the sunshine. She wondered if Luke would be back there. He had seemed so nice and she wished him all the best but it was unlikely that they would be attending church. There was never the time. Forgetting the church almost as soon as she had passed it she found a local supermarket and pulled in.

It didn't take long to do a quick bit of shopping. She even picked up a magazine and a chocolate egg with the toy inside for Abby. The supermarket had carpet cleaners so once she had done the shopping Jenny walked up to the counter.

"Are you on holiday?" a lilting Welsh accent asked her.

Jenny turned to see a woman in her 50's with a black shoulder length bob streaked with gray and friendly smiling eyes.

"No, we just moved here." Jenny held out her hand but did not know why. The woman took it and they shook.

"I'm Jenny, Jenny Evans. I just moved into Shadow Hill House with my daughter and husband."

The woman pulled her hand away and her eyes widened. Jenny wondered if maybe she didn't like strangers. Maybe she didn't like strange people moving into the area but she decided to ignore it and carry on.

"The contractors have left a few stains on the carpets. I was hoping to hire one of these, hoping they would clean it up."

"Oh, forgive me, forgive me my rudeness," the woman said. "I'm Megan Davies and I'm pleased to meet you but just a little surprised."

"Surprised?" Jenny was not sure how to take her. Maybe it was such a close-knit community that they didn't expect someone to move into the area.

"Well, you see. With the reputation of the house. No one would live there, no one's lived there for years. Not after the deaths."

Jenny felt her world tumbling away from her. Had Megan said deaths?

"What deaths?" she asked.

"Oh, it was most awful. The whole family died there but I do not know the full story. I just heard it was something terrible. They say the father went mad, killed them all he did. Now, what were their names... oh, my memory... there it is, Mary and Gabriel Pennyford. Terrible it was. Every time someone has moved in there since... well, there has been a tragedy. More deaths you see. No one has wanted to go in the house for many years. Now, let's sort you out with this carpet cleaner, shall we?"

Megan had refused to say anymore and the whole incident left Jenny feeling strangely drained. As she drove back to the house she couldn't decide whether to tell Mason. If she did he would be so angry. Not because he was scared of the house or what happened there but because he would feel they had been lied to. He would feel they had overpaid for the property if nobody wanted it. Maybe she was best to keep it quiet for now. Maybe she could even do some research and find out what really happened. After all, Chinese whispers and local gossip were not the sort of things she should be passing on. So she drove back feeling a little deflated but knowing that she would keep this to herself, at least for now. Of course, she would have to be careful, if one of the locals told Mason that could be even worse.

Caroline Clark

Chapter Four

When she got back Mason had done some of the painting and hung the blinds. As she walked into the bedroom he was just finishing off covering the stain on the wall.

"How's it going?" she asked.

"Looking good. I think this was just paint or something splashed on the wall. Fingers crossed it's gone. Now to the carpets."

Mason had hauled the carpet cleaner up the stairs and then Mason spent the rest of the afternoon cleaning the carpets. Yet the stains stayed as dark as ever. She could see Mason was getting frustrated but what could she do? They didn't have the money to replace such expensive carpets.

"Maybe we can get some rugs, and cover the stains," she said.

Mason gave her a look, *really*, it said.

She knew he was right but what other choice did they have.

The first day in the house had been spent cleaning, painting, and fixing things. Outside, Abby was having fun. They could often hear her chattering away and laughing to herself. She was still carrying that confounded bear but Jenny guessed that if it kept her happy then it didn't really matter.

It was time for tea and tonight she had cooked lasagna. This time she checked on it much more often, but even so the top was a little burnt. So she scraped off the top layer threw on some cheese and put it back under the grill. She watched it like a hawk and within just a few seconds the cheese was already melted. With the dish on the table she went to get the others. Mason was staring at the stain on the hall carpet.

"It seems to go and the minute it's dry, the damn thing's back again," Mason said.

Jenny didn't know what to say and right now she was too tired to care. They would have to cope until they could afford to replace the whole thing, until then it would just have to be covered up.

"Tea's ready and on the table, she said, "I'll get Abby, you go on through."

Silently, she crept out the door wanting to catch Abby playing. She could hear her talking and giggling to herself.

"Mr. Good Bear's not frightened of anything... no, I don't think so... I can ask Mummy." Then Abby started to giggle. It was so cute that Jenny wanted to watch her for hours and yet she knew that the meal was getting cold.

"There's lasagna and garlic bread on the table," she called out, pretending she had just got there.

Abby jumped up and turned towards her. Then she turned back as if listening. "I'll ask for you." She skipped up the step towards Jenny. "Mummy, can Victoria come for tea? She's got no mummy and daddy of her own and she's lonely."

Just for a second Abby felt her heart miss a beat. Who was Victoria? What child didn't have any parents and what was she doing here? Then she realized and remembered her own childhood and how she made up friends when she was lonely. It was normal and she decided to go along with it.

"Of course, she can, do you want her to sit next to you?"

"Yes please, Mummy, we can share."

With that Abby ran into the house holding the door as if she was allowing someone else through and then, chattering away to herself, she ran to the kitchen. Jenny wished she had that much energy and followed her through to the kitchen. Mason was already eating at the small table, so she dished up a portion for Abby and herself and sat down to join them. Abby had pulled a chair up next to her and was leaning over. The bear was on the table and the stain down the front of it was as bad as before! It looked like blood, tacky and stiff and yet when she had washed the bear the fur was soft in the water. Jenny felt a little queasy thinking of the horrid toy near the food. What was wrong with this house and why was everything stained so badly? Mason had poured her a glass of wine and she gave him a grateful smile.

"I think Teddy should not be at the table," Jenny said.

"Mr. Good Bear's hungry," Abby said.

"Well, he can sit on your knee or on the chair with Victoria."

"Why?"

Jenny rubbed a hand across her temple. The question that every parent grows to hate. Why! "You're hungry, I'm hungry, and Daddy's hungry, but we don't sit on the table now do we?"

Abby laughed at that and snatched the bear up and put him on her knee. It wasn't much better but Jenny's stomach eased with the horrid looking thing away from the food.

Throughout the meal Abby chatted away to the empty chair next to her and it really made Jenny want to smile. She looked up at Mason and could see he was frowning.

"She met a girl," Jenny said using her fingers to make quote marks. "A girl called Victoria and asked if she could bring her to tea. I didn't see any harm in it. It must be difficult for her having left all her friends behind."

Mason leaned into Jenny, talking so only she could hear.

"I'm not sure that's a good idea? Maybe we should nip this in the bud now before it gets out of hand?"

"I don't think it will do any harm," Jenny said. "Monday, she's at school and hopefully she will find some new friends."

"Good," Mason said. "I think we don't allow this friend after that."

As he said the words there was a loud crash. They both looked up to see that Abby had dropped a glass on the floor. Normally, her face would have been mortified and she would be almost in tears. Only today she looked surprised. It was almost as if she hadn't done it. Maybe she knocked it over by mistake and hadn't realized?

"Don't worry about it," Jenny said as she started to clean up the glass shards.

"It wasn't me," she said. "It was Victoria, she doesn't want to go and she doesn't want Daddy to be mean to her. She said daddies are always mean."

Jenny stopped picking up the glass and looked at her daughter. Where had that come from? She could see Mason looked annoyed but before he could say anything she interrupted him.

"Well, nobody in this house is mean and we don't call anybody that, remember?"

"Sorry, Mummy," Abby said, "but it wasn't me, it was Victoria."

"Well, if Victoria wants to say naughty things then she will have to go sit on the naughty step. If she's a nice girl she can stay here, but if she wants to say something to us she must say it herself. Okay?"

Abby nodded, picked up the bear and

ran from the table. Jenny could see there were tears in her eyes as she ran out of the room. She turned to look at Mason. There was tension in his jaw and his teeth were clamped tight. It looked like they were going to argue again. Throwing away the broken glass Jenny sat back down and took a large gulp of wine.

"You realize she's gonna use Victoria as an excuse for anything and everything," Mason said.

"You may be right, maybe I made the wrong call. Only, this has been a big move for her and maybe she will act out a little bit but let's just give her some time. Can we do that?"

Mason nodded but she could see that he was not too happy.

***

Abby had run up to her bedroom which was unusual for her. Normally, she would have gone into the living room and turned on the TV. There she would spend the rest of the night watching cartoons and playing on her tablet. Jenny realized she hadn't seen the tablet today and wondered why that was. So, she followed her up the stairs. In the beautiful pink bedroom she could see Abby playing with the teddy bear. She had a tea set with 3 cups and saucers surrounding the teapot. Teddy had one cup, Abby another and the third was opposite her.

As Jenny watched, the 3rd cup lifted into the air and seemed to float there. Her heart stopped and a lump rose in her throat as goosebumps chased up her arms.

How could this be?

Then she saw it was simply Abby. The angle of her body hid her arm and made it look as if the cup was floating. Letting out a sigh of relief Jenny walked into the room.

"Where is your tablet?" she asked.

"The internet's all kablooey," Abby said. "Sometimes it works, sometimes it doesn't, and sometimes strange things come up. I don't want to see them so I'd rather play with Mr. Good Bear and Victoria."

A different kind of fear ran through Jenny. Was Abby being targeted by online perverts? She picked up the tablet and sat down on the floor.

"Would you like to join us for some tea?" Abby asked.

Jenny nodded. "You know how much I like my tea."

Abby laughed, delighted, and got another cup and saucer from her toy box. Then she made an elaborate play of pouring tea and handing it across to Jenny. Jenny put down the tablet and picked up the cup. With her pinky finger pointed out she delicately sipped at the pretend tea.

"Mmmm, that is delicious," Jenny said.

Abby giggled. "It's a little strong for Victoria, but she still likes it."

"Maybe she needs more milk," Jenny said as she searched the memory on the tablet. At first the Internet was working and she saw the history. It was local sites, news sites. Not the sort of thing that she expected a seven-year-old to be looking at. Then she came across a story about a murder and her blood ran cold. Why would Abby find that? How would she find that? She tried to click on the link but nothing happened. It looked like the connection had gone so as she sipped her pretend tea, she tried to reconnect. Nothing was happening but she could still work out some words from the web address. They did not make her feel better. The keywords in the address include gruesome, murder, and family.

"You really shouldn't be looking at these sites," she said.

"I wasn't, Mummy." Abby looked hurt. "I think it's Victoria, I think she's trying to tell me something but I don't want to see."

Jenny felt annoyance along with a little fear. Maybe Victoria wasn't an imaginary friend but somebody online who was trying to get Abby to do things she didn't want to do.

"Remember what I told you," Jenny said. Abby looked up from her tea her eyes were wide and pleading but she nodded.

"The next time Victoria wants you to look at something you come straight to me. Is Victoria in the computer?"

Abby looked surprised and her eyes glanced towards the teacup sat opposite her.

"No, she's right here, can't you see her?"

For some reason Jenny felt disturbed at this. There was one thing with having an imaginary friend but quite another if she expected her to see that friend. She tried to search back through her memories. Had she ever expected people to see her friend? Maybe she had, maybe this was just normal and yet how had she found that website?

"Well, it looks like the tablet is not working at the moment so why don't I take it with me and see if I can get it fixed." Even though Abby didn't seem to be that bothered about the tablet at the moment, Jenny expected this to cause a major tantrum.

"Okay," Abby said her eyes flicking between the teddy and the empty place at the imaginary tea party.

Jenny decided to leave her, to go see if she could find anything on the tablet. Though she knew this was just play, for some reason she felt uncomfortable. Maybe it was just a new house, or the disturbing website. Whatever it was she couldn't shake it as she left the room.

"We're just downstairs, shout for me if you need anything."

"I will, Mummy, but we will be fine, we're just going to finish our tea."

The sound of giggling followed Jenny as she walked away down the hallway.

***

Soon, it was time for bed and Jenny went up to tuck Abby in. When she got to the room Abby was just finishing her teeth. Then she moved the toothbrush and pretended to clean the bear's teeth and then she did it to nothing. Jenny knew it was just innocent play and yet once again it made her blood run cold. *Why was that?*

Mason and her had been able to find out nothing on the tablet. First, the Internet refused to work and then when it did work the tablet just switched off. Maybe it was the battery, she wasn't sure but they were getting nothing out of it tonight. So far she hadn't unpacked her own laptop. Mason said his computer was working but he hadn't tried to connect to the Internet except for that first night when he put an advert on the chamber website. So far he hadn't checked for any replies.

Abby was getting ready for bed and as she climbed in she moved right over to the left-hand side pulled back the covers and patted the bed.

"What are you doing?" Jenny asked.

"Victoria wants to sleep with me. Is that all right?"

Jenny wanted to say no but she didn't have the heart and so she nodded. Then she quickly kissed Abby on the forehead and pulled the covers back around her, tucking her in tightly. Then she left the room, leaving the door slightly ajar.

"Just call us if you need anything, goodnight."

"Goodnight, Mummy, Victoria says goodnight too but she won't say it to Daddy."

Jenny wanted to ask why. She wanted to

say something but she was so tired that she decided to just leave it for tonight.

Jenny and Mason went to bed soon after. It was still quite early and yet they both felt tired. Once again, Mason was asleep almost as soon as his head hit the pillow. Yet, Jenny lay there listening to the sounds of the house. Whenever she went into the master bedroom she felt the air was oppressive. It was almost as if it was hard to breathe, as if there was a pressure on her chest and on her lungs. She seemed to stay awake for hours, tossing and turning and trying to listen for any strange noise. There was nothing she could put her finger on and yet she felt anxious. Why was that?

Caroline Clark

Chapter Five

The night dragged on and on and yet still Jenny could not sleep. Occasionally she would drift a little bit but the slightest noise would jerk her awake and she would be tense and listening. She would lay there as still as a corpse, holding her breath as she tried to work out what it was. It wasn't just the noises. There was something about the master bedroom that disturbed her. In her mind she believed it was simply because she was so far away from Abby. It must just be her mother's instinct and yet she knew it was more than that. The stain on the carpet disturbed her. It looked so fresh and it looked like blood. She knew this was silly but she could not shake the feeling that something bad had happened here. Maybe it was just the woman at the supermarket spooking her and yet...

The room was oppressive, the moment she crossed the threshold into the bedroom she felt breathless, and trapped. Now she lay awake, despite being exhausted, with no prospects of sleep for the foreseeable future.

What was she going to do?

Maybe it was just getting used to the house. Maybe in a night or two she would be sleeping as soundly as Mason and yet she couldn't imagine ever being relaxed in that room. It was so frustrating. This was her dream, her idea. Was it just nerves? The stress of putting their entire life into this property? She didn't know and the more she thought about it the tenser she felt and sleep receded further and further into the distance. With a heavy sigh she decided to get up. Maybe a cup of chamomile tea would help.

It was cold out of the bed and she pulled on a robe and stepped into her slippers. They had been leaving the door open, mainly on her insistence, in case Abby needed anything in the night. Jenny slipped through the door and started to walk down the corridor. It was dark, oppressively so, and she reached out with her hands to find the wall. The darkness was so deep and so black that she found herself dizzy and suddenly afraid to go any further. Hadn't she left the light on for Abby? It was something she had done both nights. Just the hall light, just so Abby could find her way if she woke up in a strange house. Maybe Mason turned it off for the darkness was an impenetrable force. It seemed to push her backward and yet she knew it was just in her mind. How silly was this, a grown woman scared of the dark?

So, she traced her hands along the wall and took tiny steps towards the stairs. It was so dark that her mind began to imagine things in front of and behind her. They were reaching out to her, claw-like fingers just inches away. Greedy mouths opening and closing with red eyes that could see as clear as day.

The sound of heavy breathing sent waves of shock through her stomach. Then she had to laugh, it was her own breathing. She was almost hyperventilating and scaring herself in the process. So she took a deep breath, pulling air deeper and deeper into her lungs and holding it there for a count of five. Then she slowly let it go. As the breath hissed past her teeth she felt herself relax and took another one. Breathe in to the count of eight, hold for five, and breathe out to the count of eight. It cleared her head and calmed her and she started to walk once more. Soon she would be at the stairwell and she decided to switch on the light once she reached it. It shouldn't wake anyone at that point, and maybe she would leave it on when she came back.

Her foot caught in something and she stumbled forward. Scrabbling in the darkness she went down on her knees. The image of a hand reaching out to grab her ankle flashed through her mind. When she hit the floor the bump shocked her and she fought to control her terror. Her foot had caught a ridge in the carpet, nothing sinister. It was just a dark house, one she didn't know but why was it so dark? Then she almost laughed again. She was a city girl. There were always street lights, and the glow from other buildings where she was used to living. She had never known a place like this. If there was no moon then of course it was dark. Slowly, she found her way back to her feet and realized she was close to the stairs. Tracing her hands across the cold wall she searched for the light switch. Just as she found it a scream ripped through the darkness.

Jenny punched the light and it flickered on. She did not know what to expect and yet she cringed and raised a hand to defend her face. There was no one behind her, no one in front. Her heart was pounding and the blood that rushed in her ears was almost deafening. What had she heard?

Then it came again and all her worries were forgotten as she raced to Abby's room. The sound was a scream, a petrified scream and it was her daughter's.

Jenny tore along the corridor as fast as her feet would carry her. All the time she was whispering, "Abby, I'm coming, Abby." Though she knew her child was too far away and could not hear her, sending the words made her feel better.

Another scream ripped through the night. It was the sound of pure terror. Was someone here? Was someone hurting her baby girl?

Behind her she heard a shout and thump. Mason was on his way. Jenny did not hesitate. Logic would have told her to wait for him but her child was afraid, maybe in pain and she ran with all she had.

When she got to the last room the door was closed and yet she knew she had left it open. Her hands found the handle and slipped in her panic.

Gripping the metal tighter she managed to turn it and the door swung inward. The sound of Abby panting filled the air and her heart leaped into her throat. She wanted to talk, to calm Abby but the words would not come. Reaching out she found the switch and the room was flooded with light.

On the bed, Abby clung to the teddy, tears running down her terrified face as she gasped for breath. The room looked as if it had been struck by a tornado. Toys, pillows, and books were strewn around the room. Jenny took it all in in an instant and raced to her daughter, scooping her into her arms and holding her close. At last her voice was back and as she stroked Abby's hair she soothed her.

"It was just a nightmare, baby, it was just a nightmare."

Abby clung to her, sobbing and shaking.

"What happened, Abby, tell me what happened?"

For long moments all Abby did was cry and cling on tight. Jenny could feel the bear between them and just for a second it made her skin crawl. Pushing the thought to one side she rocked Abby in her arms.

"Mummy's here, you're safe now. Sssssh, it's all okay, just relax."

Mason burst through the door and stopped instantly. Jenny nodded to let him know that everything was fine and he came over and sat on the bed next to them.

"What happened?" Mason asked his voice gruff with fear.

Jenny wanted to tell him to shut up, to let it pass tonight but she could see that he would not. There was heat in his eyes and even though she knew it was caused by terror and not anger she also knew it would not come across that way.

"Abby, what happened?" he demanded.

Abby pulled out of Jenny's arms and chewed on the teddy's ear. Jenny fought down the urge to vomit along with the urge to rip the sullied fur ball from her arms and burn it.

Then Abby threw her head back, her eyes wide and defiant. If it wasn't for the teddy covered in spittle she would have looked like a force to be reckoned with.

"It wasn't me, it was Victoria," Abby shouted and her eyes kept flicking to the corner of the room.

"Victoria!" Mason fumed. "You wreck your room and wake us up screaming! You can't blame an imaginary friend for this."

"I'm not," Abby snapped back.

Jenny felt her heart lurch, Abby never defied her father even if she was wrongly accused. What had gotten into her?

"Enough," Mason snapped. "I don't want to hear it."

"Stop it," Jenny whispered and she heard Mason draw in his breath. He realized that he had been shouting. She risked a glance at him and could see the blush of shame on his cheeks. He took her hand and squeezed. The gesture was an apology and an indication that she could take over. For a moment she froze. How should she deal with this?

"Daddy's sorry," she said. "You scared

him... you scared us both. We thought you had been hurt."

"I am sorry, Abby Wabby," Mason said with a smile. "I was only shouting because I thought you were hurt. Will you forgive me?"

Abby threw herself into his arms and hugged him tightly.

"I forgive you," she whispered, "but I don't think Victoria will."

Jenny felt him tense but before he could say anything she squeezed his shoulder.

"Why don't you go get a couple of mugs of hot milk and I will tuck Abby in?"

Mason nodded and left the room, glancing back at the destruction and shaking his head.

Jenny tucked Abby back into the bed and pulled the sheets around her.

"Now," she said as she started to pick up the books and toys that had been strewn across the floor. "Your dad is right. If Victoria did this then she needs to own up, where is she?"

Abby pointed to a chair in the corner of the room. As Jenny looked the corner seemed darker and she shuddered for a moment. The decision weighed heavily on her mind; should she call Abby's bluff or play along? Turning, she made her decision and raised her finger. "Victoria, if you are to live in this house then you must follow the rules."

The air seemed to chill and Jenny watched as her breath misted before her. It was gone as soon as it came and as she breathed out to check if it had happened she felt suddenly warmer again.

"If you are naughty then Mason, Daddy, will insist that you leave. Are we clear on this?"

The corner seemed darker once more and Jenny felt the hairs raise on the back of her neck. What was wrong with her? All she was doing was playing into Abby's fantasy. Yet in her mind she could have sworn she heard an angry yes.

Turning back to Abby she asked, "Does she understand?"

"Yes," Abby said, "but she doesn't like Daddy and won't be made to leave."

"Abby, that is enough," Jenny snapped.

"It wasn't me," Abby said and she threw herself back into Jenny's arms.

Suddenly Jenny felt afraid for her. "Would you like to sleep in our room tonight?" she asked.

"I don't like your room, will you sleep with us?"

Jenny wanted to ask why she didn't like their room but was afraid of the answer, so she nodded and curled up on the bed.

Mason came back with three mugs of hot milk and they all lay there drinking until Abby fell asleep.

"I'm gonna sleep with her tonight," Jenny said and she watched Mason's jaw tense.

"I don't think you should play into this fantasy, it could get out of hand."

"I know." Jenny took his hand and pulled him down for a kiss. His lips were like velvet, a sharp contrast to the sting of stubble from his chin, and he tasted of milk and honey. "Just give her a couple of days and if it still goes on I promise I will put a stop to it."

Mason nodded, picked up the cups and left. This time the hall light was definitely left on.

Jenny curled up on the bed and was soon drifting off to sleep. Just before she did she felt a figure get into the bed behind her. Assuming it was Mason she relaxed and fell into a deep and dreamless sleep.

Caroline Clark

Chapter Six

Jenny slept deeply and dreamed of an attic. There was a little girl with long blonde hair and pale gray eyes holding the teddy. Suddenly, Jenny was the girl and she knew her name was Victoria and that the teddy was Mr. Good Bear, she was hiding from the shouting. As the noise below intensified she crouched down and huddled beneath a blanket in a corner shaking and whimpering in fear. Though she could not hear the words well enough to understand what was being said, she understood the feeling behind them. It spoke of control, of dominance, and of brutality. All she wanted to do was hide and yet she wanted her mummy to hide with her. Wanted to save her and to show her this safe place. The noise below rose and fell like a bird on the thermals and she covered her ears with her hands to block it out. It was exhausting hiding, crying, and worrying about what would happen. It drained her and with each shout her body tensed as if it had been punched. Soon the tears stopped even though the fear continued. Before too long she fell asleep, all alone in a small dark room, she was so afraid.

In her dream Jenny twitched and

mumbled. Something was coming for her and she could not see what it was. She tried to hide; holding her breath, she pulled the blankets further over her head and yet she knew it would find her. Where could she go? How could she hide? For she knew if it found her that she would be dead.

Footsteps were approaching and she held her breath, willing them to go past. Step-by-step they came closer and closer. The sound of leather on the wood seemed to reverberate through her chest. With each step, she felt a small gasp of breath escape her. Though she tried to be quiet she knew she was panting and that it was too late. The monster was here, the monster had found her. The blanket was ripped from her and Jenny let out a scream, waking, just before she saw the face of evil.

Jenny jerked out of the nightmare and sat up. She expected Mason to be lying beside her. Could almost still feel the impression of a body and yet he was not there. Abby was fast asleep in front of her, and had not woken despite her scream.

Jenny sat up in the bed, it was morning and blessed light flooded the room and chased away her dreams. It all seemed so foolish in the light of day. She tried to remember the dream but it was sketchy now. There was a blonde girl with gray eyes, it must have been Victoria. The child was holding a teddy bear, the one that

Abby called Mr. Good Bear. That was the name the girl in her dream had called it. A shudder ran through her as she wondered where Abby got the name from. Surely, she must have transferred the name into the dream. It was the only logical explanation for Abby could not have known the original name of the bear.

Jenny remembered the attic from the dream and as she thought back she remembered seeing boxes of photos and old journals. Maybe she should visit the attic and see if they were there. She shook her head, just the thought of going up there was more than she could bear.

Knowing she would not sleep anymore she snuck out of bed and wandered down to the kitchen. Quickly, she made some tea and then she went into the ballroom and set up her easel. The light was perfect, bright and fresh and full of color like only natural light can be. She had every intention of painting the view from the window. It was idyllic. The sun shining down on the rolling countryside spread out like a patchwork quilt of green before her. So she closed her eyes and breathed in and then when she opened them she let her mind empty and let her arm paint. It was a technique she taught people when they got blocked. It was called free painting. So while her eyes looked at the canvas she let her hand simply paint what it wanted.

The brushstrokes came easily and fluidly to her and color was soon covering the canvas but she did not focus on the whole, just on the point that she was painting. Soon, over an hour had gone, her cup of tea was cold by her right arm. She had completely forgotten she had made it as the urge to create overtook her. Now she could hear Mason and Abby in the kitchen and knew that she had to stop, to help them make breakfast, and yet her hand painted faster and faster. The canvas was just a blur, she could not focus on the whole, just on the tiny bit that she was painting. On the startling gray of the watercolor on her brush as it glided across the canvas. Then she chose another color and again her arm and hand were not her own as they danced across the painting. This was art at its best, it controlled her, it devoured her and she let it flow through her.

"Breakfast's ready," Mason called from the door.

The words broke Jenny's trance and she put down the brush. It was a long time since she had lost herself in a painting like this and she felt euphoric and full of hope. If Shadow Hill House could give her this wonderful feeling then she knew she had made the right choice. It was the perfect place for an artist retreat.

"Thanks, honey, I'll be right there," Jenny said.

"Mummy, Mummy, Mummy, there you are," Abby said as she ran across the room. Her small feet thudded with each flat-footed step as she raced towards her.

Jenny could hear the sound of her feet on the wooden floor and she turned in time to catch Abby as she jumped into her arms. Twirling in a circle she spun her in the air before putting her down in front of the painting.

Abby drew in a deep breath and covered her mouth with her hands. Then she was laughing and pointing at the painting.

"It's Victoria," Abby said.

Jenny turned to look at the painting and her blood ran cold. Though she thought she had painted the countryside, the view from the window, the canvas actually showed a young blonde girl with malevolent gray eyes. There was a knowing smile, almost a sneer on her face and she was holding Mr. Good Bear.

***

Breakfast was bacon, eggs, and mushrooms and normally Jenny would have been ravenous and appreciative of Mason cooking. Only this morning it all looked greasy and a little burnt. Just the thought of the food turned her stomach and she had to force down every bite. Abby was chattering away to either the bear or Victoria and Mason was trying to engage in conversation but she could not take it in. All she could see was those cold gray eyes and that unfriendly smile. How had she drawn a picture of the girl, of Victoria? No matter how she tried her brain would not comprehend it. Maybe it wasn't a likeness of Abby's friend and the child had simply made the image in her mind fit the painting? Even so, that didn't explain where the girl had come from.

Jenny forced down another mouthful and had to swallow a second time as her stomach rebelled.

"Jenny, did you hear me?" Mason asked and as her mind came back to the table Jenny realized it had been for the third time.

"Sorry," she managed as she tried to push those eyes from her mind. "I must be tired, what did you say again?"

"I have been offered a job in town," Mason said, his eyes drawn together as concern lined his face. "I will be gone for most of the day. Do you need anything?"

Gone for most of the day?! Suddenly, she didn't want to be alone in the house. Alone with that girl and yet she knew it was ridiculous. It was just a painting. "No," she managed. "I'll drop Abby at school and then maybe take a look around the countryside."

"You should paint some more. That picture is so life like, it's really good," Mason said, only he was no longer aware of her mood and was back to eating his breakfast. Didn't he wonder who it was? Didn't it disturb him that she had invented a mean looking girl and painted her in a fugue state? Of course, it wouldn't, for she hadn't told him and he maybe thought it was one of the children she had met. Yet, why would she paint someone else's child and not her own?

Breakfast carried on much as normal. Abby was excited about going to school and Mason was excited about his interview. It would be good if he got a job and yet it was not what they had planned. In her dream, he worked from home. Taking on just enough clients to keep him busy and that way he was there to help her. To look after the guests and to help cook the meals. Suddenly, she didn't want him working outside of the house. Was she being selfish? A shudder ran down her back and she pushed her plate away. The food had hardly been touched and yet she could not face it anymore. It wasn't that she was selfish, it was a fear of being left alone in Shadow Hill House. Being left alone with Victoria.

***

For some reason. Jenny was nervous on

the journey back into Crick Howell, though nobody noticed. Abby was chattering away and Mason was also talking. It was good to see him excited at the prospects of work and she had to admit that an income would certainly help until she got things up and running. It would also help Mason. He had been sullen and uncommunicative. Maybe he needed this.

First, she dropped him off with a kiss on the cheek. A smile crinkled his lips and the sparkle was back in his eyes. He was expecting to be here most of the day and he would simply amuse himself in the town if he was ready before school was out. Jenny waved and turned toward the school. It wasn't much further and she soon found a place to park. As she got Abby out of the car she saw that she was holding the bear. His right ear was stuffed into her mouth and she was sucking on it. The confounded stain down the front of the bear made her skin crawl.

"I think you should leave the teddy in the car," Jenny said and watched as Abby's lip began to tremble.

"He's my friend," she said.

"I know, but soon you will find new friends and he is rather dirty still. What sort of a mum will they think I am?" Jenny knew that was a low move but she wanted to separate Abby from the toy. Only it was more than that.

The last thing she wanted her daughter to do was to sit in the corner and talk to the bear. The other kids would most likely tease her. If she had the toy she would be less likely to make friends.

Reluctantly, Abby kissed the bear and put it back on the seat. Breathing a sigh of relief, Jenny helped her from the car.

Soon she was walking past other mum's who smiled and nodded. At the gate a woman smiled and came over.

"You must be Mrs. Evans and this must be Abby."

Jenny nodded at the woman who had long brown hair and was in her late twenties. Brown eyes smiled and as she stepped forward a young girl stepped out from behind her. "I'm Julia and this is Fiona. She will be introducing Abby around today and seeing that she has a wonderful time."

Jenny let out another sigh of relief. They had a mentor for her daughter. That was such a good idea. Starting a new school was a difficult time and this would make it so much easier. Giving Abby a quick hug and a kiss she handed over her lunch box and said goodbye.

As Abby disappeared into the throng of children Jenny felt tears prickling at her eyes and turned away. There were a group of three women all staring at her and she smiled and swatted at the tears.

"Don't you worry," a brunette in her thirties with rosy red cheeks and a nice smile said. "She will be well looked after. Fi is a good child. I'm Banon and this is Awena, and Elen."

"I'm Jenny," she managed and wiped away her tears. Soon, they were talking about children and the school and they found themselves at a local café. Banon treated her to a coffee and told her all about the town. It seemed so friendly and it was good to talk to women her own age. They all had children; Banon three, two boys and a girl; Awena, just the one; and Elen had a girl and a boy.

"Where are you living?" Banon asked as they sipped on the strong coffee.

Jenny had already explained she was an artist and was setting up a retreat in the area. "We just bought Shadow Hill House," she said.

The conversation stopped dead and the three women shared a glance.

"Really?" Banon asked after several seconds of uncomfortable silence. "I never thought I'd see the day."

"I don't understand," Jenny said and

once more wondered if the locals didn't like people moving into the area.

"Ack, no you wouldn't," Elen said. She was the smallest of the three women, petite and pretty but there was a strength in her smile.

Again the three women shared a look and seemed to confer. They nodded and it was Elen who let out a sigh and began to tell the tale. "No one in the local area will go near the place," she said. "It has a history, you see. Now, do you wish to hear it?"

Jenny found that her heart was pounding and her palms were sweating on her coffee mug. Did she want to hear it? To be honest, she didn't and yet she knew she must. She opened her mouth to speak but her lips were dry and the lump in her throat would not allow words to escape so she simply nodded.

"I suppose to an outsider it will sound a little foolish," Elen said.

Jenny wasn't sure if she wanted a response or if she was just plucking up the courage to tell the story, so she smiled and nodded for her to go on.

"It was 1690 I believe, when the trouble started. There was a family living there, with one young child. I can't remember the name." She turned to her friends but they shook their heads.

Victoria, Jenny thought, *it was Victoria.*

"The legend goes that the father was a mean bully. That he beat his wife and terrorized his daughter. She took to hiding in the loft to escape him. One night, in a drunken temper he killed his wife. They say he beat her to death in front of the child. Victoria, that was her name, I remember now."

Jenny gasped as her fears were confirmed.

"Then the story is a little unsure. Some say that the child hung herself, others that he killed her. Either way, she was found hanging somewhere inside the house. He was arrested and committed to a mental asylum. However, on the anniversary of their deaths he escaped and went back to the house. It is said that he hanged himself in the same place as his daughter. Though some say it was the child. That she forced him to it and that she haunts the place to this day. The locals hate the house. Many wanted it burnt to the ground."

"Really!" Jenny said and despite the pounding of her heart, her mind refused to believe it and she didn't feel so bad. One family had died there so many years ago. They were saying there was a ghost. That was impossible, and after all, it was just 3 deaths. How many houses of that age would not have a few deaths in them?

"Oh, there's more," Elen said. "Four families have lived in the house in the intervening years. Every one of them has suffered deaths and mental illness. Usually, the father kills the family and is then committed himself, or he kills himself. You would not catch me spending even an hour in that place and I know most of the locals feel the same."

Suddenly, it seemed very cold in the café and she could see the women before her were not laughing. Part of her wanted to believe that this was some sort of hazing. That maybe they wanted to scare her from the house, and yet she knew it wasn't. Hadn't she felt strange things at Shadow Hill already?

"Which rooms did it happen in?" she asked.

Banon leaned towards her. "You've seen things, haven't you?"

Jenny shook her head. "No, of course not. It's just a big old house."

"Well, trust me," Elen said. "If you value your family's life you will leave and you will leave quickly."

Jenny found herself nodding as she

tried to stop the shaking of her hands on her coffee cup. They couldn't leave. They had nowhere to go and a mountain of debt all tied up in Shadow Hill House. Yet the thought of going back there turned her stomach. What was happening to Abby? Was it the house or just the move? Could she really let her little girl go back to that house, to Victoria?

As the ladies left, Jenny knew she had to find out more. Maybe this was just local gossip and a touch of sour grapes. Yet the house felt wrong and something was different about Abby. The ladies had mentioned the loft, she had dreamed of the loft. Picking up her keys she made a decision. She would look into the loft and see what she could find. Maybe there would be something up there, something to explain how she felt. If not, she would do more research. There had to be a logical reason for all of this.

Soon, she was back in the car and driving back to Shadow Hill. As she left the town she passed the small church. The sun was shining down on it. The quaint little building was spotlighted with glory. Maybe this was a sign. Jenny laughed, she did not believe in such things. It was just sunlight and yet where she was heading, the house on the hill was covered in shadow.

Chapter Seven

Jenny stepped into the house and was surprised that her hands were still shaking. As she glanced around the large and magnificent hallway, she no longer saw it filled with excited artists. Now she saw a malevolent little girl with dead gray eyes. Her hands were down by her side and one of them held the teddy. Mr. Good Bear. The front of the bear was splattered with blood and droplets dripped onto the carpet. Onto that confounded stain, the one that would not go.

Jenny shook her head and cleared the vision. This was just silly and yet, even though the girl was gone, the stain on the beautiful carpet was more noticeable than ever.

***

The empty house seemed to mock her. It was silent, too silent, and the atmosphere was oppressive. It was as if the house didn't want her there. For a second she turned and looked at the door. Maybe she could go back to town, spend the day shopping or in the library, and yet, that would be running. Jenny had never run from anything and she was not about to start now. She would work out what the problem was and she would solve it.

The minute she had the thought she felt better and the air seemed to clear. Maybe this was all in her head. Maybe it was just a manifestation of stress and worry. After all, Mason had lost his job, they had lost their income, and they had moved halfway across the country to a big house that had put them in debt. When she spelled it all out in her mind there was no wonder she was stressed, and it was all her fault... all her idea.

She needed to think, to work out what to do and so she went to the kitchen and ran the tap to fill the kettle. The water sputtered and then fired into the pristine ceramic sink a deep red. It splattered across the white like blood and she wanted to scream. For a moment her stomach heaved and she wondered if she would lose her breakfast. Why was she always feeling sick? Biting it down she clenched onto the sink. This house would not beat her.

In her head she imagined Mason. He was so cool and understood these things. Hadn't he told her it was just because the house had been empty for a while? Even so, she no longer wanted to drink that water. Leaving the tap running she got a bottle from the cupboard and filled up the kettle. Slowly, she prepared her teapot. Warming it with a touch of water, before rinsing that away in the sink. It looked better. The tap was running clear and there were just splashes of blood... red rust around the sides. Ignoring them she put in the strainer and spooned in two spoons of Assam tea leaves.

When the kettle boiled she added the boiling water and left the leaves to seep. Now she turned back to the sink and swilled away the rest of the rust, or whatever it may be. Seeing it made her stomach roll again but it was nothing to fear, just another problem with an empty house and contractors who failed to finish the job.

The tea was made and she picked up a newspaper and decided to have 20 minutes just chilling. The first sip of tea was uplifting and she let herself relax with the small ritual of silence, the tea, and the paper. It was good, and normal, and it was just what she needed... and yet the house was so quiet that she found it hard to settle.

Instead of reading, she was listening for noises, for anything to tell her that something was wrong... or even right. Nothing. The house was silent, outside was silent. There were no cars, or shouting neighbors, no sirens, no laughing children. How would she cope living here?

At last the tears came and she let them fall onto the newspaper and smudge the print.

Though she did not know why she was crying she knew it felt good. Just to let go of the stress and the move. Maybe it was leaving her friends, maybe it was the worry about Mason or Abby. Maybe it was that darned teddy bear or this house that was supposed to be perfect. Gradually, the tears stopped and she felt better, stronger, and she had an idea. She would go to the loft and she would see if she could find anything. So, she drank the rest of her tea and, ignoring her nerves, she made her way up the stairs.

The house was still quiet, and she tried to tell herself that it was normal. Maybe she should set her iPod up and fill the place with music. It would take her mind off things but that would have to wait. She walked down the long corridor towards their room. Whenever she came close to it she felt her chest tighten and her breath catch in her throat. Only today she did not have to go in there. Today she was going past it and that thought did not make her feel any better. As she approached the small stairs that led to the loft she felt the hairs on her arms raise. It was such a strange sensation.

As if a feather had been run along her skin, and yet it was not pleasant. Should she turn back, should she forget this or do it when Mason was here?

Then she imagined his face if she told him that she was too scared to go into the loft because her hair stood on end. Mason would laugh at her and right now she didn't think she could take that.

The staircase was built into a corner and twisted back on itself. It was done to save space but it also made it impossible to see all the way up the stairs. Jenny put her foot on the bottom step and felt her heart kick up a beat. What was wrong with her? Why was she being so childish?

Ignoring her feelings, she walked up the seven steps and then faced the wall. She could feel her jaw and shoulders tighten as she hesitated before taking the corner. It was as if she expected to be attacked. Breath held, heart pounding, she wanted to turn back. Every instinct told her this was the wrong thing to do and yet what did she expect? A ghost to jump out at her! The girl with eyes the gray of a dead fish and the evil sneer came to mind. Was she really frightened of a child? Would she let a child destroy her future, her family's future? No, she would not, she could not let these feelings stop her from investigating the house and so she stepped forward and turned the corner. Her whole body tensed and she felt herself cringe back.

There was nothing there. Just seven more steps and then a door into the attic. Letting out a gasp of air she suddenly felt better. She was behaving like a child and this was foolish. There was nothing in the house that couldn't be explained. It was just the silly women filling her head with ghost stories, that was all. It had simply set her nerves on edge.

Jenny reached the door, her heart still pounding. Though she knew she was being silly she could not seem to stop it. Her hand moved down to the handle and a gust of cold air rushed past her. Her hand froze, she wanted to turn, she wanted to run and yet she knew she could not. Somehow, she knew she had to face this but she did not know why.

Turning the handle, she pushed, but the door would not open. Then she noticed a bolt, there was a bolt on the outside of the door. Why would that be?

The only reason would be to keep something inside and yet that made no sense whatsoever. So, she slid the bolt open, having to work it from side to side as it had rusted in place. It looked like nobody had been up here for many years, or at least not for a long time.

Why haven't the contractors checked out the loft? Surely, that was one of the jobs they were supposed to do? It didn't matter now, they had gone, with no real explanation. Then she wondered, had they found the house creepy, scary? A smile came across her face. They were big burly men, what could frighten them?

She pushed the door open and darkness seemed to rush towards her. Like a shadow crossing over the sun it cooled her skin and dampened her spirits. She reached out to find a light switch and her hand scrabbled about on the wall. The darkness was so intense she felt like she was newly blind and panic rose as the switch eluded her. Fighting down her panic she reached for logic. Why had she not thought to bring a torch? Then she remembered her phone and pulled it from her pocket. Two quick shakes and the torch app came on. Hanging directly in front of her was a light cord. Pulling it, a dull yellow light blinked on and chased away the worst of the darkness.

Jenny stepped into the attic and moved towards the light. It felt safe. As if the shadows were danger and the patch of sickly light was a sanctuary. What was wrong with her thinking such crazy thoughts?

The place was filled with boxes but there seemed to be a path between them. It was covered in dust and yet the center of the path had been disturbed. It was not exactly footprints but more, as if something had been dragged across it. Jenny followed deeper and deeper into the attic until she came to the gable end. The path followed around behind more boxes, but there was a large trunk in front of them.

Jenny was drawn to the trunk and she

knelt down and reached her hand out to open it. Cold air rushed past her, lifting her hair and staying her hand. Breath held, she stood as it rose into the eaves whistling as it passed over the tiles and then came back toward her. Jenny closed her eyes and raised her hand expecting an assault. The air pushed her and sent a shiver down her spine. It chilled her skin but then it was gone. It was just a breeze, maybe from a loose tile, and it could not really hurt her.

As soon as it came it was gone and the loft was suddenly airless and claustrophobic. There was a scratching noise behind her and she turned to find nothing but boxes and shadows. What did she expect? The girl? Rats?

Admonishing herself, Jenny turned back to the trunk and bending, she reached out once more. Though she was drawn to it she really did not want to open the crate. What did she expect to see? Taking a breath she reached down once more and just as she was about to touch the crate the jarring ring of the house phone jerked her to a stand.

Feeling suddenly relieved to have an excuse to leave the attic, Jenny turned and ran. She raced down both sets of stairs and along the corridor to the master bedroom. Part of her wanted to run downstairs and pick the phone up there, but she knew she wouldn't make it. Reluctantly, she walked into the master bedroom and once again felt strangely disturbed. It was a pressure, almost like walking into a room when everyone was whispering about you. Like knowing they didn't want you there but knowing there was nothing you could do about it. She felt like the unpopular girl at school, the one no one wanted on their team. The one who was always chosen last and then ignored throughout the game. Yet, the phone sounded urgent and hearing it ring set her stomach turning. So, gritting her teeth, she walked across the room and yanked it out of the station.

***

Jenny was clutching the phone so tightly that her knuckles were white.

"Hello," she said, but her voice was barely a whisper.

"Mrs. Evans, this is the school. I'm sorry to bother you but I think you need to collect Abby. She's been very upset today and crying constantly. Something about missing her friend."

"I'm so sorry," Jenny said. "She did leave a lot of friends behind and it must be very difficult."

"We understand totally and are sure that she will settle down soon. Only, maybe today you could pick her up and perhaps she could speak to Victoria on the phone."

Jenny felt her blood run cold. Abby had no friends called Victoria... except for the pretend one.

Chapter Eight

When Jenny picked Abby up from school, she refused to say anything and just wanted to go back to the house. Only, it was not long until they needed to pick Mason up so Jenny took her shopping. Normally, Abby would have loved the trip. She could be a real little princess wanting everything and anything. Shiny object syndrome was what Mason called it. Abby would flit from one trinket to another like a bright little butterfly. Everything would delight her, everything would intrigue her and she never sulked if she was told no. That in itself made it hard to deny her and yet today she walked around the shops like a zombie. Her eyes were looking down at the ground her feet shuffled along and she stumbled every now and then.

"Let's go get a hot chocolate," Jenny said. This was another thing that would normally have Abby jumping around with delight. Only today she simply shrugged.

"Are you all right? Are you poorly?" Jenny asked.

"I just feel lost without Victoria. I just want to see her again."

Jenny took them into a café and having ordered two hot chocolates, she sat them at a booth.

"Tell me how you feel, exactly."

Abby looked up at her. There was a pallor to her skin and her eyes were dull and lifeless. Jenny's chest clenched with fear as she looked at her little girl. What was wrong with her? Was it just the move, was she missing her friends, or was it something more insidious?

"I feel weak and so lonely," Abby said. "I just want to go see Victoria. She makes me feel strong and happy and she's my friend."

"What about your other friends?" Jenny asked.

"They are not like Victoria," Abby said.

"No, maybe not, but why not ring them tonight or we can Skype them and you can talk as long as you want?"

"Victoria doesn't want me to. She says

they lie and that they don't really like me."

Before Jenny could think of an answer, her mobile phone rang and she was almost relieved to see that it was Mason.

Soon, she had picked him up and they were driving back to the house. He was excited, it looked like he had found a good job for at least a few months. The money would certainly help and yet, the first thing Jenny thought was that it was not enough for them to move out of Shadow Hill House. What was wrong with her? She wanted this move, this had been her dream for so long and now it was so close and yet she wanted to run away. Was this just her sabotaging her future? Maybe it was, maybe she was looking for problems because she was frightened of success. Or frightened of failure?

***

When they got back to the house Jenny put a cottage pie in the oven. She wanted to speak to Mason and was relieved when Abby went straight to her room.

"How was your day?" Mason asked.

Before Jenny could answer he was talking again and she could see an excitement in him that had been missing for some time. Though she wanted to talk to him, to explain her fears, she hadn't yet got them sorted in her own mind. So, she let him speak and tried to work out what she needed to say.

It seemed Mason had got a position as an accountant for a small engineering firm. The man who was doing it before him had had some accident while on holiday and wouldn't be coming back to work for at least a few months.

"Andrew, from the Chamber, thinks that by the time that happens I can have built up quite a nice clientele of my own. I think this could be a really good move," he said as he helped to lay the table. "He's already put me in touch with a few people. I think I can get my first client by the end of this week. Okay, it might be difficult for the first few months working a job and taking clients on the side, but I really do think we can do this."

"That sounds fantastic," Jenny said. She was pleased and yet worried. How could she tell him that there was something wrong with the house? That... oh, exactly what was it she wanted to tell him? The problem was she didn't know. When you tried to put it into words it all seemed like nothing. She was scared of the house, scared of the master bedroom, scared of the loft. Abby was getting a strange attachment to an imaginary friend. Was this all just in their heads or was there something more? She really wanted to ask that question, to confide in Mason and yet she feared that he would just push her fears to one side and maybe even laugh at her.

Mason continued to chat and soon it was time for dinner. He called Abby down and they sat around the table a family again. Something had definitely changed with Mason.

The confidence of getting a job so quickly had brought him back to the man he used to be. At first, the meal seemed so normal. Mason pulling faces at Abby, her sticking her tongue out at him and laughter all around the table. The longer the meal went on the more Jenny relaxed. Maybe she had invented the problems, was looking for them and therefore finding them. Maybe things were going to be all right after all.

Jenny had bought a cherry pie while they were out shopping and it was warming in the oven. Grabbing the oven gloves she opened the door to get it.

"Why were you in the attic, Mummy?" Abby asked.

Jenny froze. She could feel the heat from the oven as it hit her face and yet she felt cold as ice. How had she known? Quickly, she racked her brain going back over all their conversations. Had she mentioned going into the loft? No, she was sure she hadn't.

"How did you know I went into the loft?"

"Victoria told me. She says you mustn't go in there, that it's private, and that bad things happen in there."

Jenny felt the breath catch in her throat. Her hands were still poised in front of the pie and she knew that she must move but right at that moment she did not trust her fingers enough to dare lift the pie. With shaky hands she shut the oven door and leaned against the sink.

"Abby," Mason used his stern tone. "Don't use this imaginary friend as an excuse to be rude to your mum."

Jenny heard Mason admonish Abby but she did not know what to think. Her daughter's words went through her mind again and again. "Bad things happen in there." What did she mean? What bad things?

"I'm sorry, Daddy," Abby said.

"Tell me what bad things happen in the attic?" Jenny asked.

Abby looked as if she was talking to someone and then her face crinkled with frustration and she turned to face her mum.

"Victoria doesn't want to talk about it anymore. She said if you don't go up there you won't find out. She's not sure if she wants you to be her mummy anymore and she doesn't even want to talk to me."

"Abby, that's enough," Mason said, "now go to your room."

Abby got up and stamped her feet before walking out.

"What has gotten into her?" Mason asked with a smile on his face at their daughter's behavior.

Jenny retrieved the pie from the oven and placed it on the table. She cut them both a slice as she tried to work out what to say. Whatever happened, this was going to be a long and difficult conversation.

"I need you to listen to me and to keep an open mind," Jenny said. "There's something about this Victoria that worries me."

Jenny explained everything she could as well as she could and waited for Mason to laugh at her. He didn't. Though he didn't believe the house was to blame for Abby's behavior he could understand her worries. He promised to keep an eye out and an open mind and he promised to listen whenever she needed to talk.

It was a start and Jenny felt a weight lift off her mind. Maybe just talking about this could solve the problem. She really hoped so.

Chapter Nine

Abby had been in her room for over an hour and she had not yet asked to come out. This was unusual. Normally when she was sent to her room she would manage about half an hour and then she would come down. Her hands would be clasped together and her mouth would be closed tight. It was as if she wanted to talk but knew she mustn't. So she would clamp her lips tight until she saw them smile. Then she would say she was sorry and they would open their arms. It was the signal that she was forgiven and she would run to them and be hugged for the rest of the evening.

Jenny didn't like it that she had not followed her normal pattern. So, after an hour she crept up to her room. Abby was talking to herself but she could not hear what she was saying. It was a strange feeling but she was afraid for her little girl and a little afraid of her.

Bad things happen in there. Where did that thought come from?

Jenny listened at the door, her hand poised on the handle. Should she go in? Should she leave Abby a little longer? Then she thought about all her daughter had been through and she knew that she needed that cuddle even if Abby didn't.

Gently, she knocked on the door and stepped into the room. Abby looked angry. There was a fury in her eyes that Jenny did not recognize and she felt herself recoil from it. What was happening?

"I thought I was supposed to be left alone," Abby snapped.

"I just wanted to see how you were," Jenny said, surprised that her voice cracked with emotion and a little fear. Had bringing her child here caused this? Or was it just the inevitable stress of Mason losing his job? In many ways they had had no choice. The chances of him getting another job in London were slim and the expense of living there was exorbitant. Though he was reluctant to make the move, Mason had agreed that it was the right choice to make and now he had a job here and things were moving on. They could turn their family around and yet when Jenny looked at Abby, she saw the malicious spite of Victoria staring back at her and it chilled her to the bone. She was also holding Mr. Good Bear in front of her like a shield. The blood splattered across his front as obvious as always. For a few more long seconds they stared at each other. Like strangers fighting over the same cab on a cold rainy night. Their eyes locked and neither one would back down. Then the air seemed to crackle with static. For a moment, the room cooled and then it was like the storm had passed. Suddenly, Jenny could breathe as she saw a smile on Abby's face. What had happened? Abby was no longer the same, it was as if she was a different person. Only how could that be possible?

"I'm sorry, Mum, I don't know why I say these things, will you forgive me?"

"Always," Jenny said as she rushed forward and scooped her into her arms. Abby smelt of apples. It was a shampoo they used for her hair and it was so normal and so Abby that Jenny felt tears running down her face. As she hugged the child, she knew she had to find out what was happening in this house. Something told her she must go back to the loft, to the trunk there. She was also going to the library, to see what she could find out. Something told her the battle lines had been drawn and if she did not accept the challenge then she was bound to lose.

"You want to come and join us for a while?" Jenny asked.

"I'm really tired, can you read me a story?"

Jenny nodded and watched as Abby got ready and climbed into bed. She took Mr. Good Bear in with her and Jenny shuddered. When she sat down on the bed and placed the book between them Jenny managed to pull the bear out and toss it behind her. Maybe she could throw it away? She knew Abby would be upset but was sure it wouldn't last too long. Maybe she should just get another bear and replace this one and yet somehow, she knew it would not be that easy.

The next 30 minutes she read a story about a princess and dragons and amazing adventures. It was one they had read many times together and Abby still loved it. Just as Jenny was finishing she could see Abby's eyes closing as she fell asleep. So she read the last few words, closed the book, and tucked the duvet around her neck. Then she crept from the room only to find Mason stood in the doorway. They shared a smile and looked in on their daughter as she slept.

"How is she?" Mason asked.

Jenny didn't know how to answer. One minute it was her daughter and the next... the next it was somebody else, something else.

"She apologized, eventually. I just don't know what to make of it, or what to do."

"The first thing you need to do is have a

long soak in a hot bath. It just so happens that one is waiting for you. Along with a nice glass of wine. After all, we have something to celebrate tonight."

Jenny smiled at Mason, maybe he was right, and maybe a long soak and a glass of wine would make the world seem a different place.

Mason escorted her to the bathroom where she found candles burning all around the tub. It looked so romantic, so like the new start she imagined. A glass of wine was already waiting for her and she could see the condensation on the side which made her lick her lips. Suddenly, she wanted a drink more than anything. She turned and kissed his lips. They tasted of chardonnay, it seems he had started without her. Mason kissed her back, his mouth opening with a groan and then he pulled away.

"Just give me a few minutes to finish off and then I'll come and wash your back," Mason said and with a wink he left the room.

Jenny lowered herself into the scented water and let out a sigh. It felt amazing as the hot liquid caressed her muscles and eased away the stress. The candles created a soft and subdued lighting. Perfect for romance. Closing her eyes, she took a sip of wine and the liquid slid down her throat. It relaxed her even more.

Lulling her down into a sense of pure bliss. This was the life. This was what she wanted and this was what they deserved. They could have this and yet a nagging doubt niggled at the back of her mind. Why could she not be happy? Nothing had really happened. The house felt strange, of course it did, it was new to them. It was big, old, and cost them more than they could afford. The strangeness probably came from the fear of failure. If her artists' retreat failed then the house was too much for them.

The only other things that had happened was Abby acting out. That could be explained by the move. She was angry that she had left her friends behind and so she had made a new one. This new friend just happened to be antagonistic. It was Abby's way of coping with the move. Jenny didn't think about the people who had warned her against the house. Or the fact that Abby knew she had been in the attic. No, she pushed these things to the back of her mind and took another drink. Already she was feeling better. Tomorrow she would go back into the attic and she would have a good look around. That trunk intrigued her. Who knows what she would discover in it? Well, tomorrow she would find out. As soon as she dropped Abby and Mason off she would investigate. When she had done that she would research the house on the Internet. Who knows, maybe she could find something out that would help her gain more clients.

Closing her eyes, she leaned back in the water and took another sip of wine. This was just luxurious and she could feel herself drifting.

A hand touched her head, she knew it must be Mason and yet she was too tired to open her eyes so she let out a sigh.

The hand was cold, ice cold. It pushed down with such force that she was shoved under the water. The water was warm, the hand, being ice cold, seemed to sap her strength and though she could tell it was small she could not push back against it.

Fear filled her as her lungs gasped for air. Clamping her mouth tight she knew she must not breathe. Desperate, she thrashed in the water. Her hands reached up behind her trying to force the weight from her head. They clawed, beat, and grasped but there was nothing there. Nothing to grab onto, nothing to hold her down. With her lungs screaming, she did not know how much longer she could hold on. The urge to breathe was so strong. Kicking with her feet she pounded on the tub in a desperate effort to break free. Darkness was closing in on her and she opened her eyes and looked through the water. There was a figure above her. All she could make out was blonde hair and a twisted smile.

It was no good, she could not hold on

any longer. Though her mind knew she must not breathe, cannot breathe, her body gulped anyway. As her lips opened she took a gasp of water. The warm liquid ran down her throat just as the pressure was released.

As the liquid hit her lungs, Jenny erupted from the bath coughing and choking. There was nothing there, no one there and she crawled out of the tub and onto hands and knees.

Mason ran into the bathroom to find her coughing water out of her lungs.

Gently, he wrapped her in a towel and pulled her close.

"What happened?" he asked as he rocked her gently.

Jenny was coughing so much that at first she could not talk.

"Someone pushed me under. I couldn't breathe... I couldn't escape... there was no one there and yet I was forced under. Oh, Mason, what is happening?"

"I don't know, my love, I really don't know."

They both looked up as they heard somebody walk into the room. Abby was bleary eyed and holding Mr. Good Bear in one hand.

"Victoria says she's sorry," Abby said before turning and walking from the room.

Jenny and Mason watched her go.

"Do you think Abby did this?" Mason asked in shock.

Jenny didn't. Somehow, she knew it was Victoria and that the child was against them, or against her. It made no sense and yet she knew it. Tomorrow she would try and find out who she was. If she was a real person or if she was just a figment of her imagination. Maybe she had done this to herself? No, that couldn't be... Abby knew it had happened!

Caroline Clark

Chapter Ten

Jenny tossed and turned the night away. Her lungs burned, her throat ached, and there was a ringing in her ears that just wouldn't go away. Every time she thought she would drift off to sleep the ringing jerked her back awake. For once, Shadow Hill House was quiet. To most people it would be peaceful and relaxing and yet to her it felt like a petulant quiet. Like a child that was hiding because it didn't get its own way. To Jenny it felt as if it was waiting. Crouching in a corner and waiting for her to make a move and when she did, she was sure it would act. Maybe it hadn't decided how to act yet, exactly which side to take, but she knew it would act and she knew she must be ready.

When the alarm went off Mason got straight out of bed. It was light and the room seemed normal. Just that thought had Jenny falling asleep and she felt her eyes close and she sank into a blissful peace.

"Wake up, sleepy head," Mason called.

"Urgh," Jenny managed before she rolled over and pulled the duvet over her head. If she could just have a few more minutes then she would be able to face what came next.

Mason dressed and left the room. She was vaguely aware of him moving about and yet she still could not pull herself from the clutches of sleep until a hand touched her arm.

Jenny let out a scream and jerked upright only to look into Mason's amused eyes. He raised his right eyebrow. It had always caused her stomach to flip and her insides to melt in a most glorious way, only today she could not control the pounding of her heart and the dread that settled there.

"Would Madam like a cup of tea?" he asked and showed her the cup.

Jenny managed a smile and tried to rub strands of long black hair from out of her eyes. It didn't want to move and simply clung to her face.

"It's like a scene from The Walking Dead," Mason said as he put her cup down on the bedside table and sat on the bed.

Jenny had hauled herself into a sitting position and she took the china mug of strong Assam tea like an addict. She supped down her first taste of the malty brew and already she started to feel more human.

"Thanks," she managed and looked at

her watch. It was seven a.m., there was still plenty of time to get dressed, get Abby up, have breakfast and then the drive into town. Then she would have time to investigate. Quickly, she pushed the thoughts away. Feeling as if she must not warn the house too much in case it set a trap for her. Taking another sip of tea she wondered what Mason would think of such thoughts? Maybe, that she needed a visit to the funny farm. That was not too politically correct a name but right at that moment she wondered if it was maybe a good idea. Was she losing it?

"You need to get some sleep," Mason said with his wonderful ability to state the obvious.

"I know, I think it's just... well, everything."

"You can relax. Now I'm working it takes the strain off. In another few weeks your first customers arrive and we will be doing great. How many retreats have you got booked now?"

That thought always brought a smile to her face and yet today it hardly twitched her lips. She knew Mason saw this and she saw his jaw tighten. He was trying hard and so she let a smile come. "The rest of the year is fully booked, with a few on the waiting list in case anyone pulls out. Next year, I have the first retreat booked and will start advertising for the rest as soon as we've done with this first one."

"Not we, this has been all you, you should be proud," Mason said and he swooped down and kissed her. "Now, up you get and wake up the other sleepy head. I'll get started on breakfast."

Jenny watched him leave and felt the room darken. How could that be? She held her breath waiting for something to happen and then the room lightened again and she realized it was just a cloud passing in front of the sun. What was wrong with her?

As she dressed she couldn't tear her eyes from the stain on the carpet. It was still there and still revolted her. No matter how much they scrubbed it always came back. She made a decision. With Mason working, money would be easier. When she dropped them in town she would pick up a couple of rugs. The stain would still be there but at least she wouldn't have to see it.

As she approached Abby's room she felt the trepidation start to mount. Her palms were sweaty and her stomach was rolling. How would Abby be today?

Gently, she knocked on the door before entering.

"Morning, sweetheart," she called.

Abby was still tucked up in her bed, the covers tight around her chin with that confounded Teddy lying next to her. For a second, Jenny could have sworn it winked at her and she was filled with rage. Rushing to the bed, she stopped when she got a good look at Abby.

Her baby's skin was white and waxy and her eyes were lined with a smudged blue.

"Are you all right?" Jenny asked as she dropped to her knees feeling her forehead. There was no fever, it had to be that bear! Jenny yanked the bear from the bed and threw it to the side of the room.

Abby looked up weakly. "I don't feel too good."

"Do you want to stay in bed?"

"I'm not sure, I want to stay and I want to go to school. I will be all right." Abby smiled weakly and got out of the bed.

Jenny helped her wash and dress and all the time she said nothing. Normally, they would banter away. Sometimes Abby would want help, others, she would be all adult and wanted to do everything herself. Most days Jenny didn't help but every now and then she couldn't stop herself from hovering as she tried to hold onto her little girl. Would she ever want to let her go?

Soon they were ready and made their way downstairs. Mason had cooked scrambled eggs, bacon, and mushrooms. It smelt delicious and yet Jenny's stomach rebelled for some reason. All she fancied was ice cream but she pushed the thought away.

"How's my princess?" Mason asked.

"Not her best," Jenny said when Abby failed to answer. She shared a glance with Mason and they left it while breakfast was served and they all started eating.

Abby was picking at her meal and not eating anywhere near as much as normal. Jenny was doing the same while Mason was wolfing down his meal as if it would be stolen from him if he took too long. He reminded Jenny of a starving dog. One that had been rehomed with a good family but still remembered the old days. The thought made her laugh.

"What?" Mason asked.

"You wouldn't like it."

"Then you'd better tell me." He grinned and it cleared the atmosphere. Soon they were all talking and Abby began to eat a bit of her breakfast.

"Are you looking forward to school?" Mason asked.

"I don't want to go," Abby said, her lips curling down, her head drooped.

"Why not?" Mason pushed.

Jenny held her breath. Would she find out what was wrong? Would Abby tell him?

"I don't want to leave Victoria, I will miss her," Abby said, and this time she looked at the fourth chair at the table. The empty one.

"Well then, take her with you," Mason said and he gave Jenny a grimace. It was obvious that he knew he was going back on his own advice. After all, he was the one who said they had to discourage this imaginary friend.

"That's a good idea," Abby said jumping up from her seat and running from the room. "I will ask her."

She looked back and held out her hand, then it was as if someone took that hand and led her away and she was gone.

Mason laughed.

"I know, I'm sorry," he said. "It just hurts to see her like that."

"We can leave it for a little longer but if she doesn't let this go then we will have to do something." Jenny said the words as if she knew what she was talking about and yet what could they do?

Soon, they were ready to head out and Abby came down with her school bag. There was a smile on her face but she looked tired and worn.

"Are you sure you want to go in today?" Jenny asked.

"Victoria really wants to go," Abby said. "She's never been to school before and is really excited.

"Never been to school?" Mason asked and Jenny shot him a look. So much for not playing into this.

"No, her mummy and daddy kept her at home. She's really happy that you are here, Mummy, and wonders if you can be her parent?"

Jenny looked at Mason and could not help but laugh a little. "What about Daddy?"

"She doesn't like daddies. Maybe in time, but for now she just wants you, Mummy."

Something about that statement sent

chills down Jenny's spine. It seemed like a threat and yet Mason was pouting and laughing like it was the best joke ever. Maybe she was being silly?

Then Jenny has an idea. Maybe she could use this to her advantage so she looked at Abby. Her right hand was held out and the fingers appeared to be clasped around something. She was holding the child's hand!

Jenny dropped to her knees in front of... the pretend child, the spirit child.

"We would be happy to be your parents, but we are a family. So, if you have me as a mummy you must also have Mason as a daddy. He is very nice and a lot of fun. Just think of all the things we can do as a family." As she spoke, Jenny could feel static electricity trace up and down her arms. The hair rose on them and just for a second she could have sworn that she saw Victoria. It was just a translucent darkness, a transparent image so faint it could have been her imagination. The child was trying to smile but it came out as a sneer. Then it was gone and her mind denied it had ever happened. It was just so crazy, here she was buying into Abby's fantasy.

Realizing that she was kneeling in front of the pretend child and doing nothing she knew she had to say more. That she had to get it over that good behavior would be rewarded and that bad would not be tolerated. Yet, what could they do if she were really a ghost? Just a second after it appeared impossible the idea now seemed so plausible and yet, that in itself must be crazy. *Talk to her, to Abby via the child.* Jenny turned to Abby.

"Does she like that idea?"

Abby looked at the place she had seen the darkness and seemed to be listening. A smile lit up her face but she still looked so drawn and weak.

"Yes, she really wants to have a family and she says thank you."

Jenny wanted to ask if she was happy about Mason and yet she dare not. For some reason, she felt he was in danger and yet it was not Mason that Victoria had attacked but her. Who would it be next time?

"Well, you're very welcome, Victoria. You must understand that we have rules in the house. We will not tolerate bad behavior. You will not hurt anyone or throw toys or damage anything. You will be part of this family if you are a good girl." The air seemed to crackle and Jenny felt the hair on her arms stand to attention once more. Though nothing touched her she felt pushed backward and stumbled into a stand she moved away from the pretend child.

Was that a fit of anger? she asked herself. Had she done the wrong thing? Right then she wanted to back down but she knew that never worked. That children exploited weakness and that consistency was important. She had said that Victoria must be good and if this feeling was a show of temper then she must deal with it.

Jenny moved closer to the spot where she had seen Victoria.

"As I said, you must be a good girl or we will not tolerate you. Do you understand?"

For a second, the air left the room and was replaced with menace. The temperature plummeted and Jenny was breathing ice. It hit her lungs like a knife and made her gasp but she would not move back. She kept her face neutral and held her ground. A circle of mist left her as she breathed out and then it was gone. The air warmed and the feeling of oppression went with it.

Abby was nodding her head, looking unsure and so worried. How Jenny wanted to pick her up and hold her. To tell her that they could go back to London, back to their old life and yet she could not. She would not be chased out by a ghost even if they had a choice... but they didn't. The financial reality of the situation was that they were here for the foreseeable future and they had to make the best of it.

Abby turned to her and smiled. It was a weak smile, uncertain and a little afraid. *What was happening to her girl?*

"Victoria says she is sorry. She wants you to be her mummy and she will try really hard."

Jenny flinched a little when there was no mention of Mason but she let it slide.

"She just hates that expression," Abby said. "You must be a good girl has been said to her so many times that she hates it and it makes her angry."

"If she is a good girl then there would be no need to say it again," Jenny said moving her eyes from Abby to the spot where Victoria could be! "We would love to welcome you into our family, wouldn't we, Mason?" Jenny turned and took Mason's hand, he looked bemused but put on a big goofy smile and nodded.

Abby seemed to relax and turned.

"We best get ready for school," she said. "Victoria is really looking forward to it."

With that she held out her hand and skipped from the room. It looked so strange and yet so normal and Jenny let out a huge gasp of air and almost collapsed into a heap.

Chapter Eleven

Jenny dropped Mason at work and then took Abby to school. All throughout the journey she was talking excitedly to herself.

"You will make friends," she would say. "Yes, you will have fun. The school was always fun back at home. No, I don't want to go back, well, maybe sometimes but not to leave you."

Jenny found herself both amused and a little worried.

"Did you meet any new friends?" she asked.

"No, not really," Abby said. "One girl called me strange for staying at Shadow Hill."

"Well, if she does it again you tell the teacher."

"I can't snitch," Abby said in a voice way too old for her seven years.

Jenny found herself laughing and worried all at the same time. How difficult must it be starting a new school in the middle of the term?

She parked the car and helped Abby out grabbing her bag and then her hand out of instinct. Abby pulled away.

"Mummy, Victoria had that hand!"

"Oh, I'm sorry, Victoria."

Jenny stepped around Abby and took her other hand. It felt wrong, dangerous. Abby was now closest to the road and every nerve in Jenny's body rebelled and yet she did not know what else to do.

Soon, they were at the school gates. Jenny bent down and handed over a lunch box. It contained two sets of sandwiches, two cake bars and two apples. She hoped that Abby would not make a fool of herself in front of the other children but what could she do. Bending down she kissed her cheek.

"Have a great day," she said and was about to go.

"Don't forget Victoria's kiss," Abby said.

Jenny looked around, no one was paying any attention so she ducked down again and kissed where she imagined the child was supposed to be.

"Have a great day... both of you," she said before watching Abby run through the school gate her right hand held out to the side.

Oh, what was she going to do?

***

Jenny wanted to run back to the house to start looking into the loft and yet she also dreaded it. So she nipped into the shops to look for some rugs. Both carpets were rich and deep in color. The hallway, a busy red and deep blue pattern and the bedroom, a rich burgundy. What she needed was a rug that wouldn't look too out of place and she spent an hour looking backward and forward between the rugs until an exasperated sales assistant tracked her down.

"Can I help you?" he asked.

Jenny wondered whether to explain the situation and in the end decided it was the best way. So she told him off the stains and the problem. He steered her to the back of the store where offcuts of carpet had been made into rugs. They were perfect. There were some very similar to the hallway.

In the end she picked one a little darker

for the hallway. It was red and almost black but she hoped that in the shade it wouldn't look too bad. For the bedroom she picked a slightly lighter color. Thinking that it would brighten the dark room and add a bit of warmth.

Feeling much more positive, after all, the house would not beat her. She would hide these stains whether it liked it or not and feeling much better she headed back to Shadow Hill.

Once there she intended to rush straight up to the loft and begin her investigation. For some reason she was drawn to it. Maybe it was because Victoria had warned her out of there, maybe it was her dream, or maybe it was that trunk. It didn't matter, until she went back up it was like an itch that she couldn't quite reach.

Yet, she wasn't quite ready so she put on the kettle while she got the rugs from the car. The first one looked much better than she could have hoped. Yes, it looked slightly out of place, especially if you were near it but from a distance it was hardly noticeable. It was much better than the angel shaped stain.

Grabbing the other rug she hauled it up the stairs to the bedroom. As she turned the corner she stopped. There was a figure stood there leaning over the balcony just above the stain. Her mouth opened and she tried to shout but then it was gone. It faded before her and melted into the wall. What was wrong with her?

The rug had dropped from her hand and she wondered whether to run or to carry on. For a moment she thought about going, and yet where would she go? So, she picked up the rug and, denying her fear, she walked on to the bedroom.

As always, she felt her skin crawl slightly as she entered the room, but she shook it off. *You're not driving me out*, she thought and walked in with her head held high.

The stain in this room was at the base of the bed.

Jenny dropped the rug and arranged it so that it covered the stain. It looked good and as if it was meant to be there. She wondered if Mason would even notice it, she knew he no longer saw the stains. What was it with men?

Leaving that age old question for another day she went downstairs and made a cup of coffee.

The kitchen was so quiet and so perfect. It was a combination of old and new and was exactly what she wanted and yet if felt alien. The coffee had gone cold and yet she could not force herself to leave this room. Somehow, she felt safe here and was trying to build her courage to face the loft and yet it would not come.

This was ridiculous, she had so much to do before her first clients arrived. There was a bedroom to paint, as well as part of the hallway and their own room. Once that was done she needed to complete a few works to demonstrate with. She had pencil drawings done but she wanted to do the same bowl of fruit from conception to completion and use it to train her students. It was quite a bit of work and she had waited until they got here as she wanted to complete the painting in the room she would use to train. It made a difference what light was used and this would be the most authentic she could get.

Then she had to set up her paperwork for the course. She had started to develop notes and workings but they needed completing and printing out. Then she wanted to do a welcome pack. Again, this had been left until they were here so that she could see the house first and make sure that everything was right.

Then she realized that she hadn't been online since they arrived. Most of her correspondence came to her phone and that had been blessedly quiet but she should check her email accounts to see if there were any emails and queries and she also wanted to look into the next advert.

All of this was waiting for her and here she was twiddling her thumbs because she wasn't sure whether to open the trunk of an imaginary girl. If that wasn't procrastination at its greatest, then what was?

Somehow, that thought broke her reticence and she found a torch and set off for the attic. If there was anything to find she would find it and she would get to the bottom of this mystery.

Once more, as she approached the bend in the stairs, she felt her heart kick up a beat. What did she really expect to find behind that wall? A vision of Victoria filled her mind and she shook it away. After all the ghost was at school with her daughter. That was a really crazy thought and she knew it. After she had climbed the seven steps she hesitated before turning. Listening, she tried to discern if anything was waiting for her and yet all she could hear was the ringing and hissing that had plagued her since her encounter in the bath tub.

What had that been? Was It Victoria? If so, what did it mean?

Jenny found she could not make any sense of it and so she pushed the thought aside and wondered what she should do if the spirit came back. If something had really attacked her in the bath then they were obviously in danger. What else could it have been? A panic attack? Could she have slipped and panicked so badly that she felt she was being attacked? It didn't make sense, she was not like that and she decided that as soon as she was finished here she would get on the internet and see if she could discover any way to protect her family.

Taking a breath, she turned the corner to find nothing. Just the seven stairs up to the white painted door with the lock on the outside!

Taking the steps quickly, before her nerves could get the better of her, she flicked on the torch and pulled open the door. Darkness escaped and stormed the stairwell. Jenny flinched back as if it could harm her. The thought of that gloom touching her skin tightened her chest but she shrugged it off and stepped upward. It was just a shadow after all.

With the torch she found the light pull instantly and this time the sickly yellow glow seemed even weaker. It was just a glow in the distance and she was surrounded by shadows and yet the torch pointed the way. It shone directly where she went the time before, directly back to the trunk.

Jenny looked around, scanning the beam over the boxes and other items that were so covered in dust that they appeared as just shapes. They hulked at the edge of the beam and she was waiting for their eyes to open and the shapes to move. To become living, breathing monsters. What was wrong with her?

Though she was an artist, she had always recorded what she saw, not some fantasy world. In fact, she had never believed in anything that could not be seen and recorded and surely this spirit was neither of those. Only, she had recorded it and she had seen it. Suddenly, she could picture the painting in the ballroom and the fear was almost overwhelming. Pulling to a halt she wondered about running from here and never coming back. Only, she must find out what was going on. Mason wouldn't. He didn't see things the way she did, didn't feel the trouble with Abby. If she gave in now then they were at this... this... thing's mercy.

Ignoring the way her heart thumped against her chest, ignoring the ringing in her ears, she inched forward. With each step she searched the darkness. Looking for anything that may lead her to an answer but there was nothing. Just more junk, more clutter and lots and lots of boxes.

The sound of panting stopped her and she strained to hear. Was someone here? Each time she stopped to listen the sound stopped. She would strain for any sound but nothing was there so she let out her breath and moved again. The panting was back and it was so close. Jenny pressed a finger to each ear, for a moment, the ringing stopped and she listened. All was quiet, no one was here unless they were watching her, following her and stopping each time she stopped. Panic was like a beast inside her. Clawing its way through her sanity as it tried to escape. Only the thought of Abby kept her here and kept her moving. This time, as the panting came back she recognized it. Her own desperate hyperventilating had been scaring her. There was no one here but her and her panic.

Moving forward again she was almost to the box. The air seemed thicker now. It was harder to breathe and she had to fight hard to control the panic. To force herself to take long, slow breaths because she was starting to feel faint. Slowly, just breathe slowly and deeply, she told herself and the room cleared.

Then she stopped before the trunk. It was surrounded by boxes and she could see that a path led behind them. What was there? She knew she would have to find out but first things first. This trunk had called her and now she was here would she have the courage to open it?

It was an old-fashioned shipping trunk. Dark wood bound with metal stays. The lid came over the box and had a catch that could be secured with a padlock. The metal was old and looked to be green with oxidation. Jenny paused but she knew she could not stay here too long, if she did her nerve would surely leave her. It was time, she reached out her hand and moved it towards the trunk. There was no blast of air this time and yet an almost imperceptible current ran through her hand. It wasn't quite static but there was a buzz in the air. As if the trunk was repelling her but its batteries were wearing low.

Was that because Victoria wasn't here?

Pushing such a foolish thought away she touched the lid. Again there was no shock but a definite current. A feeling of malevolence filled her and she pulled her hand back.

"Oh, stop this," she said to the empty attic and the words reverberated in the eaves and came back to her. That was creepy but was explainable, or at least she thought it was. The room was just flat surfaces with no carpet or wallpaper to deaden the sound waves.

Again she reached out, this time the current was even less and she did not pull her hand back. The trunk buzzed slightly beneath her fingers and then it was still. Slowly, with gritted teeth she lifted the lid.

It was full of dolls. Their lifeless gray eyes all staring up at her. Then she realized they were the same dead fish color of Victoria's eyes. Most of the dolls were blond too and they were as creepy as dolls can get and yet she imagined they were old. As she picked one up she expected it to move, or to try and bite her. It did nothing, of course, it was just a doll. The face was hand painted porcelain she thought and very well done. The dress was exquisite, the stitching perfect. For some reason, she reached in and pulled out another and another and then she saw books beneath it. They were journals, all leather bound, it looked like four of them. With a shaking hand she pulled one out and what she read on the front chilled her blood.

This Journal Belongs to Victoria Pennyford

Aged 9 Years

The Year of Our Lord 1690

Victoria had existed. Could Abby have come up here and found this? Was that why she imagined Victoria as her friend? Jenny found so many questions going through her head she wanted to scream at them to stop. Where had she heard the name Pennyford?

The cover sent ice water through her veins and once more she was breathing too fast and coming close to a panic attack.

Shutting her eyes, she took a deep

breath, and then she opened them and skipped through the journal.

Mama and Papa are fighting again. The screams resonate through the house. I heard Mama say that was why my room was so far away. I know I must stay in my room when Mama screams, but it is so hard. The monster came again last night and I was so afraid.

Jenny read more, it spoke of a terrified child and an abused mother. It seemed the woman was trying to protect her daughter but still the abuse was overwhelming the child. Jenny felt tears running down her cheeks as she felt for Victoria and all she had been through. She turned to another page.

Papa sent me to the loft again. I have made my own place and brought a blanket up when he wasn't looking. Sometimes I play with my dollies but it is so dark and the monster hides up here. I hear him whistling and know he is coming for me. I am so afraid that I hide under the blankets and keep as still as I can. That way the monster will miss me, or at least I hope so.

As Jenny read the words she heard the wind whistling. It worked its way through the tiles and whistled between them before escaping further down the attic somewhere in the eaves. She could understand how a terrified child would think it a monster. It certainly made her own heart pound a little harder.

Jenny skipped on more and more of the pages. Each time she stopped to read, the journal told of a girl afraid of her father and how she wanted to help her mother. The further towards the end the more the girl hated her father.

She was beginning to see him as the monster and yet she couldn't quite make herself accept it. Then she found a dozen pages that looked strange. She stopped and read them.

I must be a good girl. I must be a good girl.

I must be a good girl. I must be a good girl.

I must be a good girl. I must be a good girl.

I must be a good girl. I must be a good girl.

I must be a good girl. I must be a good girl.

I must be a good girl. I must be a good girl.

I must be a good girl. I must be a good girl.

There were over 10 pages all with the same words, all neatly written. No wonder Victoria didn't like that phase! Now, how could Abby know that? Either she had been up here or she had communicated with Victoria somehow. Jenny kept looking through and there were more instances of it. The next time there were over 20 pages, all so neatly written and yet in places the paper had crinkled. It looked like Victoria had cried when she wrote this.

I must be a good girl. I must be a good girl.

I must be a good girl. I must be a good girl.

I must be a good girl. I must be a good girl.

I must be a good girl. I must be a good girl.

I must be a good girl. I must be a good girl.

I must be a good girl. I must be a good girl.

I must be a good girl. I must be a good girl.

Time after time she came across the same phrase that filled page after desperate page with the same awful words. How could the poor child have coped with this? There was more about her being locked in the attic. At least, that explained the lock on the outside of the door. It was not to keep something evil in, just a poor frightened child.

There were times in the journal when Victoria had been struck. Times when she had been screamed at, or dragged up here by her hair after her mother had been knocked unconscious. Jenny wondered why the woman didn't leave him but then she realized that 1690 was a different time. How would a single mother cope with a child in those days?

Jenny couldn't read anymore. It made her feel ill that a parent could do this to his daughter and she could understand Victoria's animosity towards Mason. What child would want a father after some of the things that hers had done to her?

She put down the journal and followed the track between the boxes. Though she knew what she would find it was still a shock. Victoria had built a room out of boxes, there was just a small entrance, like an igloo, and Jenny shone the torch down the hole. She could see a blanket, another journal and a children's book. There were bits of candle wax on the floor and she could see a candle stub in the tiny room. Though there was no way she was going in there. It was way too creepy, she could empathize with Victoria. The child had made the best of her situation. She was clever and resourceful and brave. The thought of her using a candle amongst all this paper was terrifying. How could anyone do this to a child?

Jenny turned and she heard the house phone ring. Today it didn't scare her. Instinctively she knew it was the school. That there was trouble with Abby and that she would have to come home again. How she hoped that this new knowledge would enable her to help Abby and she realized that she also wanted to help Victoria.

Though her mind rebelled against it, she believed that Victoria was a spirit child and that she was stuck in Shadow Hill House.

Maybe all the stories those women had told her were true. Yet, Jenny could not feel angry at Victoria, the child had suffered and she was fighting back in the only way she knew how. Jenny had to find a way to help her or destroy her. Somehow, she had to do that and at the same time keep her family safe. Was such a thing even possible?

Chapter Twelve

Jenny drove to the school a little too quickly. It seemed that Abby had assaulted another pupil and the school was adamant that she was brought home immediately. When Jenny got there she could feel their stares. They think this was caused by bad parenting and maybe it was. Maybe they should have put a stop to this situation some time ago but how do you do that?

In the end all Jenny could do was apologize and explain that nothing like this had ever happened before. Gently, she took Abby's hand and led her from the school. Once she was in the car she let out a sigh of relief.

"I'm so sorry, Mum, but it wasn't me... it was Victoria."

As soon as the words were said the car cooled and the air filled with menace. Jenny could see her breath frost before her and she felt crushed by Victoria's intent. How was the spirit doing this? Shouldn't it be tied to the property? Keeping calm, she knew she had to reassure her own daughter. Victoria was scared and suffering but so was Abby. Jenny turned in her seat and smiled.

"I know, sweetheart, and I believe you," Jenny said. "Victoria, if you are listening to me, I understand what you have been through and I want to help you. We need to talk, to communicate, and I want you to trust me. No one will ever hurt you again, I promise."

The air warmed and the pressure felt easier.

"Now, I'm going to drive us home but we can talk on the way. Abby, if Victoria tells you anything you can tell me, I believe you, honey, there is no need to hide anything."

Abby nodded and Jenny turned back and pulled the car out of the school yard. She could feel the accusing eyes of fellow students and she wondered if her daughter's school career could ever recover.

On the journey back Abby spoke about the day.

"Victoria didn't like the other girls," Abby said.

Keep calm, Jenny told herself. "Do you

know why?"

"Because they were nice to me. She's really angry with you as well, Mummy," Abby said and Jenny could hear the tears in her voice. She really wanted to pull over and hug her daughter but she felt that it was best if this was kept dispassionate for now. It seemed cruel but she was scared of upsetting Victoria even more and having this escalate before she was ready to handle it.

"Do you know why?" Jenny asked and yet she knew why. She had violated the child's diary.

"You went to her secret place and she doesn't like it."

"I know I did, Victoria, and I'm sorry. The reason I did it though was because I want to help you. I want to understand what you have been through and I want to help you get over it.

Jenny felt the steering wheel yanked to the right and she had to fight to pull it back. The car swerved and lifted onto two wheels for a moment but luckily, the roads were clear and they did not hit anything coming in the other direction. Adrenaline flooded Jenny's body, causing her heart to pound and her arms to prickle. These was a pressure on the wheel, someone was holding it and could turn it at any moment. Which way would she go this time? Would Jenny be quick enough to stop her?

"Do not get upset," Jenny said. "I'm not trying to make you leave." She didn't know why she said that but it seemed to be the right thing and the pressure on the wheel lessened and then was gone. So, it looked like the spirit was afraid of being banished. She could understand that but one way or another she had to go.

The rest of the drive was uneventful and Jenny was relieved when she pulled up into the driveway. Abby climbed out and they walked into Shadow Hill House. Jenny expected it to feel different, expected a presence, or malevolence and yet there was nothing. The magnificent hallway greeted them, filled with sunlight, it seemed to glow. The throw rug covering the carpet was barely noticeable and they walked past it and into the kitchen. If she didn't know what was happening it would look perfect, just like she imagined it.

Jenny sat down at the table and indicated for Abby to join her.

"Victoria wants to play outside," Abby said.

"We should talk first." Jenny pulled out a chair and waited for Abby to sit down.

Abby pulled out another chair and

placed Mr. Good Bear on the table. *Where did he come from*, Jenny asked herself as she was sure the bear was upstairs. The bloodstain seemed to mock her and for a few moments she could not pull her eyes from it. *What had happened to the bear and was Victoria holding it at the time?*

Abby sat down in the chair closest to Jenny and looked at the other chair. For a moment, Jenny expected to see it move. The thought of the ghost child pulling the chair under the table was almost too much for her. This whole thing was crazy, and yet it was happening.

"Tell me what occurred today," Jenny asked. "I'm not angry and you are not in trouble but I need to know the truth."

Abby was staring at the empty chair, her fingers holding on to the crusted fur of Mr. Good Bear's stomach. For a moment, Jenny wanted to scream but she knew she must be patient. She had to let this play out and to learn from it what she could. Now, Abby was nodding and mouthing as if she was talking to someone but was making no sounds. How long would this go on? What would happen to her little girl? At last Abby turned towards her.

"Victoria doesn't want to go to school anymore, she wants to play outside."

"First, I need to know why," Jenny said as gently as she could manage.

The room cooled, not enough for her to see her breath but enough to feel it. Victoria was getting angry again so she must tread carefully.

"I can only help you if I understand. Do you hear me, Victoria?"

The temperature raised a little and she could see that Abby was turned away from her again, intent on the empty chair.

"Victoria doesn't trust anyone. People can be mean and hurt you. She just wants to stay here with me."

That was worrying, not with all of them, just with Abby.

"We don't want to be mean to you, Victoria. We want you to be part of our family... but to do that you must understand what we need too."

Once again the room cooled and Jenny felt as if the air was getting thicker, heavier. She must tread carefully.

"We need you to talk to us, to explain how you feel and let us help you. We also need Abby to go to school she must learn her lessons for if she does not we will get into trouble. If Abby doesn't go to school then the authorities will come and that could be bad for all of us. Do you understand?"

Jenny could see her breath frosting before her and it felt hard to breathe. It was obvious that Victoria was angry but she was not prepared to back down, not fully. If she let the spirit know that she was weak she felt things would be worse.

"Victoria says she will think about it but we have to play outside. Can we go now?" Abby asked.

The last thing Jenny wanted to do was let her child go outside with this spirit and yet she felt it was maybe the right thing to do for now. Still, she hesitated.

Across the kitchen, on the surface, the toaster flew to the end of its cord and then snapped back and landed with a heavy clatter on the counter. It was as if an angry child had slammed it across the worktop. For a few moments it jiggled at the end of the cable, banging up and down as if someone was picking it up and dropping it. Jenny knew she was beaten. Letting them go out and play was possibly the only thing she would be allowed to do.

"Of course you can. Go outside and play

but don't go too far. I will bring you out hot chocolates in about half an hour so stay close."

Abby jumped up and grabbed the bear. With her right arm held out as if she held someone's hand she ran from the room.

The toaster dropped back down onto the countertop and was silent and still. Jenny let out a gasp and flopped onto the table. With her head in her hands she wanted to scream but she knew she mustn't. She had half an hour to do some research and then she had to check on Abby. Who knows what could happen if she left it any longer?

Chapter Thirteen

Jenny sat at the table wondering what to do. Part of her wanted to run out of the door, grab Abby, get in the car and drive so far away that she would never think of Shadow Hill House again. Yet she knew that was not possible. Another part of her even felt sorry for Victoria and wanted to help the child find peace. Yet, just thinking that made her wonder if she was mad. Had she lost it? Had the stress of the move and their finances pushed her over the edge? Only that didn't explain Abby and the trouble she was in. It didn't explain what was happening in the house. No, there was more to this and Jenny had to find out what it was.

So, she found out her laptop and logged onto the Internet. Mason had told her it was only working occasionally and she expected it not to work now. Could Victoria be the reason it wasn't working? If she was, surely she would not be able to search for ways to destroy the spirit child.

Only, the Internet was working and it was reasonably fast but that didn't help Jenny much. When she searched for ways to get rid of a ghost most of the websites were rather foolish. The other ones she found were for books only they were fiction books. What did you do if you had a real haunting?

Ghostbusters.

As the word came into her mind she had to laugh. Only, that was what she needed. A real life ghost buster. Maybe the priest could help?

Ignoring that thought Jenny changed tactics. She searched for true ghost stories, and real haunted houses. Most of the results were rubbish and yet one stuck out to her.

The Haunting of Seafield House a True Story from a True Skeptic.

At first she thought it was another book but the link took her to a blog written by a woman called Gail Parker. It appeared that Gail was engaged to a man who believed in spirits and invited her to a haunted house. Jenny read the blog, scouring down the information like a blind man who suddenly had sight.

Gail had not believed anything she had seen. In fact, at first she blamed it on an illness but soon she could not deny what was going on all around her.

When Jenny read that it was a child who was haunting the house she felt her blood run cold and thought of Abby and Victoria. She checked her watch, it had been three-quarters of an hour since Abby had gone out to play. Though she wanted to read more, to research more, and possibly even to contact Gail, she felt that she had left it too long. If Victoria was frightened or feeling threatened, who knew what she would do. Quickly, she bookmarked the page and closed the laptop. Hopefully, Abby and Victoria would be just outside. She could check on them quickly and then come back in and do some more research.

Jenny left the house hoping to see Abby on the lawn at the back. It was a large stretch of open grassland with wonderful views all around. There was nowhere to hide and yet Abby and the teddy bear were nowhere to be seen. Jenny felt her heart kick up a notch and her breath caught in her throat. Had something already happened?

Part of her wanted to run back to the house and call Mason. Only he couldn't get back unless she went to fetch him. There was no way she was leaving the house, not until she had found Abby. Trying to calm the panic that raged in her mind she wondered where the child could be. Maybe she had just wandered around the house or around the grounds.

Fighting down her panic she set out to search.

The house was surrounded by grassland and gardens. It was all low growing with no shrubs, or trees, or buildings where a child could hide. There was also not much to do except to sit on the grass and play. That was truly what she had expected Abby would be doing. Playing with that confounded bear and her pretend or spirit friend.

Shadow Hill House sat on a hilltop and most of the land for miles around was easily visible and truly picturesque. Perfect for artists. If Abby had gone in all but one direction then she would be able to see her. There was just one side of the hill that was covered with woodland. Had Abby ventured into those trees? Jenny doubted she would have felt safe to do so. As a city girl she was used to streets and cars and people. Surely, the dark and lonely woods would seem a scary place. They certainly did to Jenny!

Approaching the trees Jenny fought down her panic and started to call out.

"Abby, Abby where are you... Abby?"

The words were absorbed by the trees and seemed to travel no distance. Jenny was running up and down the side of the woodland. Where would Abby be? How would she find her if she had gone into these woods?

It was darker under the trees and to Jenny it seemed so very scary. There were no birds singing and the trees seem to murmur a warning. In her mind, she could hear them telling her to keep back, keep back they whispered and rustled, keep out, keep away. Only it must all be in her mind. Panic clawed at her mind and stomach making her nauseous and uncertain what to do. One moment she wanted to call the police, the next Mason, and the next Gail Parker. How would she find her? What should she do?

Just when she had decided she must return to the house and call the police she noticed a path. It was little more than trampled down grass and looked as if it had not been used for a long time but it was clearly the only entrance into the woodland.

Caroline Clark

Chapter Fourteen

Without even thinking Jenny stepped beneath the trees and followed the path. It was darker under the branches and cooler. Not as cold as the house when Victoria was angry but maybe she couldn't affect such a large area so deeply. Jenny shook her head, of course it was cooler, the trees blocked out the sun. Further and further she followed the path and soon she was running. Her breath was coming in short sharp gasps, tears ran down her face and she thought that she was wailing just a little.

All sorts of images flashed through her mind and none of them were good. Who would take a child into a woodland? What would they do with her there? The best case scenario was that Abby was taken by a ghost and yet how could that ever be good?

Suddenly, Jenny turned a corner and stopped instantly.

Abby was there in a small clearing. The

bear hung from her left hand. She was mercifully alone and staring at something in front of her. Jenny ran to her side and grabbed her by the shoulders. Abby let out a squeal and jumped away, turning, her eyes were wide and frightened.

"It's okay, baby, Mummy's here."

Abby ran into her open arms and Jenny hugged her tightly. As she held her to her chest she looked over her shoulder and almost let out a gasp of her own. There was a gravestone sat alone in the desolate clearing. Though the writing had worn on the stonework it was clear what it was. What was Abby doing here? Jenny shuddered. How had her baby found this place and who did the grave belong to?

"What are you doing here?" Jenny asked as she pulled back. Abby had tears in her eyes. They were wide and pleading and her bottom lip trembled.

"Victoria lives here," Abby said. "She wanted me to see this place. She wants me to live with her but I want to stay with you, Mummy, and Daddy. Victoria says you can maybe come with us but that Daddy can't because daddies are always mean."

Jenny felt as if a knife had been plunged into her heart. The spirit child wanted to kill her baby, to put her in the cold dark ground and keep her here forever. Jenny pulled Abby to her chest once more and hugged her tightly.

"Well, you're staying with us," she whispered into Abby's ear. "Victoria can be your friend but she cannot take you from us. Now, let's get you back to the house with a nice hot chocolate. Would you like that?"

Abby nodded against her shoulder.

Jenny did not know what else to do but she knew the stakes had been raised. As quickly as she could, she walked her away from the graveyard... gravestone. Only her mind would not come away. Was the grave really Victoria's? If so, why would she be buried here? Jenny knew she had to come back to find out but for now she would have to pick Mason up and give her heart and mind time to settle. She had to learn how to keep her baby safe and what to tell Mason.

Daddies are mean... should she involve him?

If she did, was she signing his death warrant? Even though she knew the thought was crazy it made sense and she knew she must keep this to herself for a little while. So far, Victoria seemed to have ignored Mason and maybe it was best if things stayed that way.

***

Abby soon seemed to forget her fear and worry and once she had drunk her hot chocolate her spirits were fine once more. The journey to fetch Mason went uneventfully. He had had a wonderful day and couldn't stop talking about it. Though Jenny wanted to tell him her fears and what she had found on the Internet she held her peace. Even though she wanted his help and support she still thought it was better if he knew as little as possible. He would fight for his baby... if he believed her... and that could spark Victoria to remove him. So, Jenny listened to Mason and let the normality of his day offer her some piece.

Once Mason and Abby were back in the house Jenny asked for half an hour just to do some drawing. Mason was pleased to let her go, happy to see that she was interested in her art once more.

So, Jenny left the house with an art pad and pencil and traced the route back to the graveyard. Once more the trees seemed to be whispering, and warning her, and yet this time she could hear birdsong. Maybe she had before, only maybe before, her panic was so bad that she had simply shut it out. For a moment or two she just stood and looked at the grave. The gray stone was worn and pitted and the writing had faded so much that it was illegible. Only there was a way to read it and that was the reason she had brought her pencil and pad. Before her courage left her Jenny tore out a sheet and placed it over the gravestone. Taking the pencil, she ran it backward and forward across the paper until she had a rubbing of the cold gray stone. What she saw chilled her to the bone. With her breath coming in desperate gasps, she pulled off another sheet and completed the same task on the bottom of the stone.

Stepping away from the grave she looked down at the two sheets of paper. The world seemed to spin before her and darkness closed in. For a moment, she thought she would faint but she bit down on her lip and as her mouth filled with blood the pain brought her back to the present. Slowly, she read the rubbings off the gravestone

Victoria Pennyford. Born 1681

On the second sheet it read.

Died 1690

Buried here in unhallowed ground.

All she could see in her mind was the journal.

This Journal Belongs to Victoria Pennyford.

Aged 9 Years

The Year of Our Lord 1690

If this was Victoria's grave, how did she end up here? Why was she buried in the unhallowed ground? What did it all mean?

Chapter Fifteen

Suddenly, the woods darkened, the birdsong stopped and a feeling of oppression came over Jenny. Something was wrong. The trees were whispering to her but she couldn't make out the words. Maybe it was hurry.

Then she knew that Abby was in danger. It was simply an instinct, maybe a mother's instinct, but it was strong and she knew she must get back to the house. Turning from the grave she picked up the papers and ran.

"I'm coming, Abby," she called at the whispering trees as she stumbled along the track. It was darker now, as if the trees were menacing her but she would not stop. "You keep away from her, you bitch," she called as she raced back to the house.

Jenny burst in through the door shouting and calling out Abby's name.

"What is it?" Mason called as he ran

from his office.

"I just have a feeling... A terrible feeling. That Abby is hurt."

Together they turned and ran to the stairs, as they passed the throw rug neither of them noticed the stain that had soaked through from the carpet.

They both reached the top of the stairs together, turned to the left and raced along the hallway. Jenny wanted to call out but she was desperate for breath. It seemed she wasn't fit enough for this so she simply ran as fast as she could. When they arrived at Abby's room the door was closed. As her hand touched the handle she felt a mild shock and pulled away quickly.

"What was it?" Mason asked, but before he waited for a reply he pushed her aside and grabbed the handle himself.

By the way he jumped, Jenny knew he felt it too. Something was trying to keep them from their daughter's room and she prayed they were not too late.

Mason didn't hesitate, he squeezed the handle tighter and pushed the door. It gave slightly but then slammed back closed.

"Abby, what is going on?" Mason

shouted.

"It's not Abby," Jenny said before she thought to stop yourself.

Fortunately, Mason wasn't listening to her and tried the handle again. This time he leaned into the door with all his strength. For a moment, she thought it would not give, that they would be locked outside of the room while Victoria devoured her child. Jenny could feel her breath coming faster and faster and knew she was beginning to panic. Once more she bit down on her lip, the pain steadied her.

"Help me," Mason said, and so Jenny added her weight while he tried to open the door. She could feel the pressure pushing back against them. It was way too much for one nine-year-old and then it gave. The door slammed back and bounced on the wall revealing the darkened room.

Jenny ran in. There was clutter all over the floor; books, pillows, a chair, and other things she could not recognize. Ignoring the mess she raced to the bed to find Abby lying there, her eyes closed. Jenny feared the worst for a moment. Was she too late? Was Abby already dead?

"What's going on in here?" Mason asked as he picked up things from the floor and pulled back the curtains.

The light should have flooded into the room and yet the gloom was hardly lifted. However, it gave enough of a glow for Jenny to see that Abby was breathing, albeit very shallowly. She put a hand to her forehead. It was cold and clammy. Gently, she shook Abby and saw her eyes open.

"Hey, baby, how you feeling?"

"My tummy hurts and my head is all like candy floss only painful," Abby's voice was little more than a whine.

"I think we should take you to the doctor's." Jenny leaned down to pick her up but before she could the pressure in the room grew and she saw her breath misting before her.

"What's happening?" Mason barked. "How did it get so cold in here?"

Jenny stopped, not sure what to do. Would Victoria let them leave? Yet, as soon as she had the thought she knew she had to try. Abby was fading, she was very ill, somehow she knew that if she didn't get out of here that she would die. Moving as slowly as she could she put her arms around her. Before she could lift Abby a book flew from the floor and crashed into her shoulder. The pain was not as bad as the shock and the force that pushed her backward.

"What the..." Mason shouted, his eyes were wide and questioning. "How did that just happen?"

Jenny knew it was time to tell him but she also knew they didn't have the time.

"We have to get Abby out of here, Mason, help me."

She could see that Mason was unsure, that he wanted to question her, but maybe there was something in her expression which stopped him. Instead, he nodded and moved towards the bed. The table lamp shot off the bedside table and sailed through the air. Jenny kept expecting it to get caught on the cord and to pull up sharp, only it didn't. When it hit the cord it simply hesitated and then ripped it from the wall and carried on its journey before it smacked into Mason's head.

He staggered backward and was fighting off books, brushes, and glass ornaments. The ones with the snow scenes inside that Abby loved so much. They were all flying towards him. Bit by bit Mason was pushed out of the room in fear of his very life. Jenny reached down to grab Abby. The pressure in the room was getting worse and worse. It felt as if her lungs were bursting as if she couldn't draw air and yet she knew she must.

"Stop this!" she screamed. "Just stop

this. We said we would look after you but only if you behave."

For a second, the pressure eased but then it was as if the wind whipped up inside the room. It grew and grew until it felt as if a tornado had landed there. The force of it pushed Jenny towards the door. Try as she might she could not resist it and she could see Abby further and further away as the undetectable force pushed her across the room. As well as the invisible wind, Jenny was getting battered with books, ornaments and debris. Though she fought to stay in the room, to stay close to her baby, she was gradually pressed out of the door. As she crossed the threshold she saw Mason. He was lying in the hallway, blood running from his head. Jenny turned to reach for him and the door slammed shut. Victoria had separated her from her baby. Now what was she going to do?

All Jenny wanted to do was scream but she knew she had to stay calm. Bending down she reached out to Mason and tried to find a pulse. His eyes opened and he pulled himself up to sit against the wall.

"What happened?" he asked and rubbed at the cut on his head.

"Abby is in the room with Victoria, we have to get her out of there."

Gently she touched his head. The wound had stopped bleeding and though it would cause quite a bruise it wasn't too bad. Mason was staring at her, he clearly did not understand.

"Who's Victoria... you mean the imaginary friend? Something was going on in there, something that wasn't our little girl."

Jenny put her hand on his cheek and looked into his eyes. As always the gesture calmed him, steadied him.

"I want you to listen to me. I don't know how much time we have and I don't know what to do. You need to listen to me and to try and keep an open mind."

Mason nodded.

Jenny swallowed, she was still gathering her breath and she did not know where to start. Panic was like a beast inside of her and if she let it, it would take control. Only she knew that would not help anyone, least of all Abby.

"I know this is hard to believe but I think Victoria is a spirit child. She wants Abby to come and live with her. Earlier, I found Abby in the woods. There is a grave there. It belonged to Victoria and carved into the stone is the fact that she was buried in unhallowed ground. I do not know what that means but I know we need to do something."

Mason nodded and indicated for her to continue.

"I've been doing a little research."

"How long have you known about this?" Mason asked, and she could see his jaw was tensed, his eyes challenging her.

"The house has felt wrong to me since the day we arrived. At first I thought it was just stress but more and more things have happened. I don't have time to explain now but Victoria wants Abby to live with her. I think she means to kill her, to turn her into a ghost."

"What can we do?" Mason asked.

"Stay here and try to keep Victoria busy but be careful, she hates daddies."

"I don't know how," he said, and she could hear the fear in his voice.

Jenny wanted to scream, she wanted to scream at Victoria, at Mason, at the unfairness of all this and yet she knew there wasn't time.

"Just do something, I have an idea, maybe it will work, maybe it won't but it's all we have. Try and keep our baby safe until I get back." Jenny pulled his face towards her and kissed him on the lips, before turning and running down the hallway.

The fear inside her was like a living thing. Here she was, running from the house, not knowing if she would ever see her little girl again. Was she making the right decision?

Chapter Sixteen

Jenny ran down the corridor to the sound of Abby screaming. It took every ounce of resolve she had to keep moving, to run away from her child.

"Victoria hates you, Daddy, she hates you, and she wants you to die. If you don't leave she will kill you."

Jenny sobbed at the words but she must keep running. She was no help here.

Grabbing her keys from the kitchen she raced to the door and then into the car. The engine revved as she gunned the pedal, the wheels slipped on the driveway. Though she knew she was panicking she could not ease up and pushed the pedal even harder. At last the wheels bit and the car tore away towards what she hoped would be their salvation. The roads were narrow and twisty and she knew she was driving too fast. As she approached a corner she suddenly realized where she was. The road turned back on itself at almost 180° and she was going way too fast. Her foot hit the break and she hauled on the steering wheel. The car leaned over, the tires screeched on the tarmac. For a moment she was on two wheels. Had she blown it? Would she end up dead in the dike while she left Mason and Abby to their fate?

The car seemed to hang in the air forever but it could only have been less than a second before the wheels touched the blacktop and they surged forwards. Jenny knew she needed to slow down, to be more careful. Crashing would help no one.

As she drove she tried to remember what she had read on the website. It was something about an exorcism. Was she crazy? Would anyone believe her, would he believe her? It didn't matter right now, he was her only hope and so she pushed the car as fast as she could and prayed that she would make it in time.

In less than 15 minutes she pulled up outside the small church and ran from the car. Before she knew it she was hammering on the door of the rectory and wishing with all her heart that the young priest would be here.

At last the door opened and she let out a gasp of relief. It was Luke Jones, the young priest. His eyebrows knitted together with concern as he reached out towards her.

"Mrs. Evans, Jenny, are you all right?"

"I... I don't know... I need your help. Abby, Abby, my daughter, is in danger and I don't know where else to turn."

"Come in and sit down. I will make some tea and you can tell me all about it." Gently, he put a hand on her arm and tried to lead her into the house. Jenny shook the hand away.

"We don't have time. I know you won't believe me but she is in grave danger. My beautiful little girl is in danger and you are my only hope."

Tears started to fall and Jenny knew she was close to hysteria. If she did not stop it then she would be a wreck and if that happened he would never believe her.

"What can I do for you?" he asked.

"I need you to come to Shadow Hill House. I need you to bring your Bible and holy water and I need you... I need you to exorcise a spirit."

"I'm sorry, Mrs. Evans. I'm truly sorry but we don't do that, not anymore."

"You believe in good?"

Luke nodded.

"Then you must believe in evil. I'm begging you, come with me even if you don't believe me... bring whatever you have and come with me and see what is happening. My little girl's life depends on it."

Luke stood for a moment thinking it over and then he smiled.

"You are right, that house does have a most unfortunate history, now just give me a second and I will come with you. I am not saying that I believe you but who knows, maybe I can help."

Jenny was flooded with relief and she started sobbing once more.

"There, there, don't you cry, now everything will be all right."

"Please hurry, I know you think I'm distraught but please, just hurry."

Soon, they were on the way back to the house, only this time Luke drove. Jenny was frustrated with the speed at which he was driving.

For such a young man he was like an old lady behind the wheel and she found her knees were tapping and she was sighing and groaning constantly. The young priest took no notice and tried to keep her talking.

"Explain to me what happened," he said.

Jenny took a breath and tried to think of everything that had happened so far. It was not easy as many of the things were so small and insignificant that they wouldn't sound real and yet she had to try.

"It started the minute I arrived, this was my dream, and had been for years and yet the moment I walked into the house I felt that something was wrong." Then she explained about the imaginary friend, the house going cold, the pressure, the stains, the flying books and lamps, what Abby was saying and at last, she told him about the gravestone. "Why would a child be buried in unhallowed ground?"

"Usually, such a thing is reserved for criminals, and even then, it is normally those of the nastiest kind, usually killers."

"She's just a little girl, how could that be? How could she kill somebody?"

"There is another possibility, if it was thought that the child had committed suicide, then it is possible that the local church would not allow her to be buried in the churchyard. We don't do that anymore. Our Lord is a forgiving God"

At last, they arrived at the house and Jenny hoped that they were in time, what would she do if they were too late?

Chapter Seventeen

The moment Luke walked into the house Jenny could see that he felt it, the presence, the ghost. Whatever it was that was causing these problems, the young priest picked up on it and she saw the expression on his face change. There was a seriousness she had never seen before and a determination that boded well.

"Take me to the child," he said.

Jenny nodded and led him into the house. As they started to walk up the stairs they could hear screaming and there was something else. Jenny started to run, it was Mason and he was in trouble. Without waiting for the priest she ran along the corridor and just hoped that he would follow. What she found almost dropped her to her knees. Lying on the floor his face blue, his eyes bulging was Mason. His hands clawed at his throat and he was gasping for breath.

"What is it?" she asked as she knelt down beside him.

Mason's mouth opened but no words came out and his hands scratched at his throat drawing blood. Tears were running from Jenny's eyes, she did not know what to do as she watched her man fading before her very eyes.

Luke arrived behind her and crossed himself. Opening his Bible he began to read. Jenny looked up at him her eyes desperate.

"Help him," she pleaded. "Please help him."

Luke nodded and carried on reading.

"PATER noster, qui es in caelis, sanctificetur nomen tuum. Adveniat regnum tuum. Fiat voluntas tua, sicut in caelo et in terra."

Jenny reached down to Mason's throat, though she could see nothing there when she touched his skin she could feel the coarse hemp of a rope. It was strong and tight around his neck. So tight it was strangling him. That was what he was clawing at, that was what he was trying to release.

As Luke continued to chant she felt the rope slacken.

"Panem nostrum quotidianum da nobis hodie, et dimitte nobis debita nostra sicut et nos dimittimus debitoribus nostris. Et ne nos inducas in tentationem, sed libera nos a malo. Amen."

Beneath her fingers it melted away and then it was gone. Mason drew in a deep breath and then began coughing. The coughs wracked his lungs and shook his body but she could see that his color was returning to normal. There was blood on his throat and on his fingers and a deep welt raised on the skin of his neck. It was only then that she became aware of Abby shouting in the other room.

"Victoria hates you, you must die. Men are evil, they are not welcome here, leave or die. Leave or die, leave or die."

Over and over again she shouted out the words but Jenny didn't care, for now, at least, Mason was safe.

The priest closed his Bible and helped Mason to his feet.

"Let's get him downstairs and away from the power of the spirit. Then we can talk and I will see what I can do for you."

Jenny nodded and between them they took an arm each and helped Mason to his feet. Though his breathing was easier now, she could see he was still weak. Slowly, they led him down to the kitchen and sat him in a chair. While Jenny stood beside him Luke found a glass and poured him some water.

"Sip this slowly, it will ease the pain and help."

Jenny took the glass and held it for Mason, her hands were shaking but already she could see he felt better. Whatever Luke had done had saved them... for now. If he could save Mason, surely he could save Abby."

Mason sipped at the water, coughing occasionally, but he was looking much better already.

"I think you should leave the house, Mason," Luke said. "It appears the spirit is against men and I feel it would be safer if you were outside."

"That's my little girl up there," Mason managed, his voice croaking badly. "I can't just leave her."

"You won't leave her," Jenny said. "I will be here and so will the reverend. Maybe it would be better if you were outside anyway, maybe she will be less antagonized."

Luke was nodding. "That makes sense, and along those lines, I think we should carry on this conversation outside. Who knows how far she can hear, we do not want to tip our hand."

Mason put down the glass and stood and they all walked out of the house. Luke led them several hundred yards away from the property and then sat down on the grass. Jenny thought he did this because he was worried that Mason would not be able to stand for long and she was grateful to him.

"There are things I have to tell you," he said. "Each Diocese has what we call the Diocesan Deliverance Team. This is a team containing a priest with special training and another with psychiatric training. Their job is to come into situations like this and assess them. Most of such occurrences can be explained by simple psychiatric disorders."

Jenny could not listen to this any longer. "How can you say that this is a psychiatric disorder?"

"I didn't, I said that most such occurrences can be explained that way. In this instance I believe we have a vengeful spirit. Now, I am part of the Diocesan Deliverance Team for this area. Officially, I should speak to the deacon and seek the help of the psychiatric priest before I go any further." He raised his hands to stop Jenny interrupting once more.

"I understand, in this circumstance, that that would be foolish and could cost lives. What I want to do is talk to the spirit with prayer, under most circumstances that will persuade her to leave. However, I strongly suggest that Mason stays outside. I am happy if you both stay outside, but that is up to you."

"I want to come with you," Jenny said. "I cannot leave my baby in there alone."

"I was hoping you would say that, however, if I ask you to leave you must do so, instantly and without any arguments."

Mason stood and hugged Jenny to him.

"Be careful in there," he said, and then he popped his phone into her pocket before pulling away.

Jenny and the priest went back to the house, before they entered, he stopped her.

"I intend to pray, this time it well be the Lord's Prayer in English, before, I did it in the Latin and I may do so again but I think the English will work fine. This is about intent and staying strong. I will also be using another prayer. While I am doing this I want you to talk to the spirit child. I know you will want to talk to Abby but it is important that you don't. Tell the spirit child it is okay to leave, that there is nothing to fear and that you care for her and would not tell her such things if you did not believe them. Can you do that?"

Jenny nodded though she knew it would be hard. If Abby was frightened she wanted to tell her it was all right and yet she felt some sympathy for Victoria too. Something awful must have happened to her, otherwise she would not still be here.

Together they walked back into the house.

As they came close to the room she could hear Abby crying. There was no other sound, just the lonely and sad crying of her young girl and it tore out her heart. Luke squeezed her shoulder and opened his Bible and began to pray.

"OUR Father, who art in heaven, hallowed be Thy name."

"Victoria, you know how much I care for you and I hate to see you suffer," Jenny said, and all the time the crying of her daughter was like a knife to her heart.

"Thy kingdom come. Thy will be done on earth as it is in heaven."

"It is time for you to leave, but do not worry, you are going somewhere wonderful," Jenny said, despite wanting to break down the door and hug her baby.

A shriek of pain and anger came from behind the bedroom door.

Jenny ran to the door but Luke stopped her. He held his finger up to his lips but all the time continued praying.

"Give us this day our daily bread and forgive us our trespasses as we forgive those who trespass against us."

Jenny was fighting down her own tears and trying to control her voice. She knew she must not let Victoria know how angry and worried she felt and yet it was almost impossible.

"I have been talking to the local priest, he knows all about you now and he knows what happened to you. That is why he is here to take you somewhere nice, somewhere where you can relax and feel love and joy."

"And lead us not into temptation, but deliver us from evil. Amen."

The sobbing from behind the door had stopped but the hallway was darker and Jenny felt the hair on the back of her neck stand on end. A shadow crossed over them and it prickled the skin on her arms. The air was charged and it felt as if something was coming, something was about to happen. She looked at Luke, he felt it too but he shook his head and continued praying. Suddenly, the room was cold, so very cold that their breath misted before them. Jenny rubbed her arms and wondered about Abby, was she scared? Could she help her? Though she wanted to rush into the room and hold her she knew she must trust the priest.

"Visit this place, O Lord, we pray, and drive far from it the snares of the enemy."

"You can trust me," Jenny said. "I want only the best for you and this life is lonely and painful it is not what you want. It is time for you to go, to leave us. We will not forget you, we will visit you and bring you flowers and you will be at peace."

The air was heavy and hard to breathe, the darkness seemed deeper and the feeling of malevolence made Jenny want to run. What must Abby be feeling?

"May your holy angels dwell with us and guard us in peace, and may your blessing be always upon us; through Jesus Christ our Lord. Amen."

"Do not be afraid," Jenny said. "You can leave this awful life, you can leave this place and find the love that you have always wanted. It is there waiting for you and will surround you as soon as you let go."

Jenny felt the air ease, she could breathe and as she took a breath and let it go she noticed the misting, the chill was gone. Little by little the room seemed lighter and she knew that they were winning.

"There is a home for you, be brave and go to it and know that love will find you. Our love will help you there." The words were hard to say and she hoped that Victoria would not take Abby with her, what could she do to stop that?

Luke nodded his head in encouragement. "Through Jesus Christ our Lord. Amen," he said his hand on his Bible.

The door to the bedroom opened. This time, Jenny couldn't stop herself, she ran into the room. Abby was sat on the bed, there were tears in her eyes and she was holding Mr. Good Bear but she looked like their daughter again. Jenny pulled her into her arms and hugged her tight, kissing her head and her hair.

"Are you all right?" she asked.

Abby wiped away the tears.

"Victoria was frightened and she got really mean, but she's gone now. She was my friend but she's gone."

Jenny squeezed her a little tighter.

"She has gone to a better place and you will soon find new friends, I promise," she whispered into her ear.

Caroline Clark

Chapter Eighteen

It was if a depression had been lifted off the house and suddenly, the sun was shining. The following morning Abby couldn't remember anything and she was no longer holding the bear. That in itself made Jennifer feel better and she grabbed the thing as soon as Abby wasn't looking and consigned it to the rubbish.

Mason's throat was red and raw and his voice was scratchy and hoarse. Jenny dropped Mason off at work and Abby at school. She went in and spoke to the teachers and though she didn't mention what had happened she said that there had been some problems and that they were resolved now. The teachers were happy to give Abby another chance and simply moved her to a different class. There they found her a new mentor, a girl called Gwyneth, who would look after her and see that she found friends. When Jenny left she was pleased to see that Abby was smiling and laughing. It looked like they had survived and that it was all over.

Jenny drove back to the house and started working on the course material for her artist's retreat. She spent the whole morning and was so engrossed that she didn't realize what time it was until the phone rang. For a moment, her nerves jangled along with the bell. Was it the school again? Was Abby in trouble?

Leaving her work, she crossed to the phone and snatched it from the base station.

"I just thought I'd see how you were doing?" Mason said.

It was great to hear his voice, even though it was still very croaky.

"I'm doing great. I've done most of the coursework for my first retreat. Oh, and when I left, Abby looked to be having such fun at school."

They talked for another 15 minutes and to Jenny it felt as if this was the first time they had talked openly and so freely since Mason lost his job. Things were going fantastic and she could not wait for the future. It was only four more weeks until her first retreat and she knew she had a lot to do.

By the time the weekend came the house was more normal. There'd been no more talk of

Victoria and Jenny no longer felt as if it was rejecting her as if there was a presence. At the weekend they decided to walk into the woodland and explore the local countryside. It was a beautiful day and though Jenny never said anything, she deliberately walked in the opposite direction to the small path that she had found. They spent a few hours walking in the woods pointing out birds and a squirrel and all the different trees for Abby. It was peaceful. Jenny and Mason held hands as they walked while Abby skipped ahead laughing before running back with something she had found. The first was an acorn, then some sycamore seeds, and then a branch that was twisted until it looked a little bit like a rabbit. Just when they were about to turn back they came upon the grave.

Jenny felt her blood run cold but this was not a supernatural chill. It was simply the fear of bringing back the bad memories and how Abby would react.

Abby ran towards the stone and got down on her knees.

"What is this?" she asked, her face all innocent inquiry.

It was obvious she didn't remember coming here and Jenny wasn't about to remind her.

"It's just a stone marker, unfortunately, the words are worn away so we can't read it. We must be nearly home, come on, I'm hungry, aren't you?"

"Can we have cheese triangles and toasties?" Abby asked.

Jenny was so pleased that Abby hadn't remembered, she could see that Mason was confused but she decided to tell him later. The last thing she wanted to do was mention Victoria, especially in this place.

Soon, they were back at the house and everyone had cheese on toast for lunch. Abby went to her room to finish up some school work and Mason sat down with Jenny at the table.

"What was that stone?" he asked. "I saw you go white and I saw you watching Abby like a hawk, was that something to do with Victoria?"

Jenny nodded but there was a lump in her throat and she had to swallow it before she could speak. The last thing she wanted to do was remember what happened. Since the day of the exorcism the house had seemed so bright and so full of laughter and love. The last thing she wanted to remember was the darkness and feeling of control and terror that came with it. Yet, she knew that Mason deserved an explanation. Knowing him he wouldn't stop until he had one.

"That was the grave of Victoria Pennyford, the spirit child that was haunting us. If you remember, I told you she was buried in unhallowed ground. That was the grave. I found Abby there one day... well, that was the day when she was taken so ill. Today, I feared I would lose her again. I was so afraid that if she recognized what the grave was that it would bring it all back. Luckily, she doesn't seem to remember."

Mason nodded.

"We were so lucky you went to that priest. I don't know what happened but I know things have changed and it is over. Even the stains, the one in the bedroom and the one in the hall, they seem to be fading. I think if I run the carpet cleaner over them again they will be gone."

"I hope so," Jenny said, and yet somehow, she felt uneasy. Seeing the grave had changed things for her and she could not shake the feeling that something was coming.

Later that night when she was all alone she went back to the research she had found on the Internet. Once more, she looked at Gail Parker's blog and read what she had intended to read before. The stories were fascinating and terrifying all in one go. However, there was lots of good information. Things to arm herself with in case this was not over.

It seemed that the spirits fed on fear and negativity. It powered them and gave them strength. The more strength they had the more control they had over the real world. While some spirits were looking for peace, others were simply destructive. Those of the latter persuasion were very difficult to get rid of. They would hold on to what they deemed was theirs, and though they may be weakened, if they were ever invited, they could come back. After a couple of hours of reading, Jenny decided to email Gail and tell her about the house. She was very surprised when she got an email straight back.

Gail, along with her partner, Jesse, were researching as many haunted houses as they could. They had made a career out of it and would be happy to come and investigate if she needed it. However, they were currently looking into another house, one that was in Scotland and so it would be a couple of weeks before they could get there. What she did suggest was that Jenny researched the house. That the more she knew about it the more she would know how to deal with it. Before she could reply, Mason came through with a glass of wine and so Jenny sent back her thanks and called it a night.

Mason sat on the sofa and Jenny sat with her legs across his as they both sipped at their wine.

"Are you ready for the first visitors?" Mason asked.

"As ready as I'll ever be." Jenny laughed. "Though I can't believe how nervous I am. This is my dream, and yet now I would do almost anything to not have them coming." It felt so good to them to talk about normal things and to be able to laugh and joke with no dark presence looming over them. Mason couldn't fully understand the difference but she could tell that he felt it.

"You will be fine, I've seen the paintings you've done, they're fabulous. Your guests will be blown away."

Jenny hoped so, that her dream was finally coming true and that the ghost wouldn't be able to ruin it for her.

Soon, they went into the bedroom and Jenny no longer felt threatened as she crossed the threshold. The throw rug she had bought ended up having to be thrown away. Blood had somehow soaked through it from the stain on the carpet. Yet now, as Mason said, the stain was fading. Maybe she would go into town and pick up a carpet cleaner again, maybe this time both of the stains would go. With that thought in her mind she lay down to sleep and yet all she could think about was researching the house. There was nothing on the Internet and so she decided to go to the library tomorrow. She could do that at the same time as she picked up the carpet cleaner and then maybe she would call in to see the priest. So far she had never got around to thanking him and she knew she should have.

Though Mason often played it down, she really believed that without the man's help, that Abby would be dead now. Maybe she would be haunting them too, haunting them with Victoria. Jenny shuddered. Before she drifted off to sleep she could not get rid of such a terrible thought. Her little girl trapped in this house forever. Driven mad with rage and grief and suddenly she felt truly sorry for Victoria. However, if the spirit ever came back for her daughter then she would destroy her. All she had to do was find out how.

Chapter Nineteen

The following morning Jenny drove Mason into work and then dropped Abby off at school. She made a quick stop at the supermarket to pick up some shopping and the carpet cleaner and was driving back to Shadow Hill House. As she passed the little church she decided to pull in and see if the reverend was there.

She pulled the car to a halt and felt suddenly guilty. This should have been done before. It was so easy to come here in a panic when she needed help and yet she had not returned to give her thanks. The vicar had put his faith in her, he had listened when he didn't need to. More than that, he had acted and she could not thank him enough for it. Yet she could not pluck up the courage to get out of the car until a knock on the window had her jumping out of her skin.

Turning, she saw Luke's smiling face and she grinned back at him.

"Why don't you come in for tea?" he said through the window.

Jenny nodded and followed him into the rectory.

It was a neat and tidy, if old fashioned kitchen. Jenny sat at a small oak table. There was a large pink chrysanthemum in a pot in the middle of it and she stared at the flower while he made the tea.

Soon he placed a teapot, 2 cups, milk, and sugar on the table and sat down with a smile on his face.

"It is so good to see you," he said. "I've wanted to call around but was not sure that I could face coming near that house again. I do hope you'll forgive me?"

Jenny felt her mouth drop open and for a moment she did not know what to say.

"It is I who need to apologize," she managed. "I have wanted to come and thank you ever since that night and yet somehow I've never felt able. How do you thank someone for what you did? Whatever I came up with seemed so insignificant."

"The fact that you have faith in me is enough. Can I ask, has the spirit gone?"

"Yes, it has, and Abby has returned to her normal self. She seems to have very little memory. Though she sometimes asks where Victoria is, she does not seem able to remember who she is or where she saw her."

"And yet I suspect there is a but," Luke said as he poured the tea.

Jenny took the little china cup from him and smiled. The kitchen, the tea, the plant, everything reminded her of an old lady's house and yet the priest was a young man. Maybe this was just the way he found it?

"I just feel that it will come back, that she will come back. Victoria! It is as if I am waiting for the worst to happen. I've been talking to a lady who has been through something similar and she suggested that I research the house. I've been to the library but there isn't much there and I wondered if maybe you could help me?"

This time it was Luke who stopped to take a sip of his tea. Jenny could recognize it as a delaying tactic only because she had just done the same. She could see him thinking, weighing up the pros and cons and she wanted to press him but decided it would be better to let him come to his own conclusions. Yet, she hoped that he would help. At last, he put the cup down and looked at her.

"I have been doing some research in the church records. They are quite extensive and go back to that time. The house was owned by the Pennyfords, Mary and Gabriel. It is true that they had a child called Victoria."

Jenny felt that sick feeling come over her and her blood ran cold. Even though she had been through all of this, part of her still hoped that it was just her twisted imagination. That Victoria never really existed.

"I see," she said. "Did you manage to find out any more?"

Once again, Luke seemed to hesitate. He poured them both another cup of tea. It was strong and probably not as warm as it should be and yet he sipped his gratefully. Jenny picked up her cup and she had to grip hard to stop the china cup rattling in the saucer. Quickly, she took a sip and let the lukewarm liquid offer her comfort.

Luke put down his drink as if afraid he would drop it and raised his eyes to her. There was fear there, but also determination.

"From what I can gather, Gabriel murdered Mary in a fit of jealous rage. The records aren't extensive but I believe the local vicar thought that he was abusing her before it happened. In those days, there was very little he could do about it. I do believe he spoke to the man but it did not do any good. Gabriel was committed because the murder was so horrific, he stabbed her so many times... in the bedroom, I believe."

Jenny felt herself shudder. The stain on the carpet and across the wall. Was that where Mary had died? Of course, it was, but who was powering the stain? Victoria or Mary? Then she wondered about the stain in the hallway.

"I have heard rumors that Victoria was hanged in the hallway. Can you tell me if that is true?"

"I have found out very little about the child. There is a record of her birth and there is a mention of her death and that she was not allowed to be buried in the churchyard. Only that is all I could discover. I wish I could have been more help..." his words trailed off and he looked down at his hands.

"I see," Jenny said, and yet she felt a deep sense of dread. Was this over?

"I will keep looking and let you know if I find anything else."

Jenny managed a smile and yet she felt as if she was waiting... but waiting for what?

***

Days turned into a week and then two and nothing more happened. Mason's confidence was growing and soon he was back to the sweet and tender man that she had married.

There were no more strange occurrences and yet Jenny was constantly waiting, but waiting for what?

Abby was enjoying school and had made some friends and really, everything was perfect. Yet, Jenny would spend several hours each day researching online. It was as if she could not let it go and yet she knew it was more than that. Day after day she went back to Gail Parker's blog and each time she would see the Skype button. For long moments, her mouse pointer would hover over it and yet so far, she had not pressed it. Once again, she could not pluck up the courage and so she slammed the laptop cover closed and went back to her painting.

In the ballroom she had set up a canvas and a pallet of paints. When she returned she found both of them on the floor. Panic rose in her chest like flames. She was turning, backward and forward, looking for trouble. The hairs on her arms had not raised, the room had not darkened, and the air was pleasantly warm. What had caused this? Then she saw the curtains fluttering in the wind. The window was open. It could have been something as simple as the breeze. Jenny retrieved the paints and sat down to finish the last of her examples for her retreat.

After an hour she took her brush and slashed a big brown X across the painting. It was terrible. The perspective was wrong, the light was wrong, and the whole thing looked worse than a child's first try. For some reason she couldn't concentrate and she knew she would get nowhere until she resolved it. Closing her eyes she let her mind empty. For the next two minutes she thought of nothing. Every time a thought intruded she pushed it aside and just let her mind clear. Only one thought would not go. That was Victoria. Even though the child was gone she needed to know why she had been here in the first place. It seemed silly but somehow, she knew she would have no peace until she understood. Opening her eyes, she went back to the laptop. Though she knew the chances of Gail answering her Skype were slim to none, she finally plucked up the courage to press the button.

The call was answered almost immediately and Jenny found herself looking at a woman in her mid-20s. She had long brown hair, kind brown eyes and though she was a little on the slim side, a friendly smile. She recognized Gail Parker from the photo on the website and spent the next few minutes explaining who she was. Gail had remembered her from their earlier email.

"One thing I really need to know is why she was here? Why was she haunting this place and what did she want?" Jenny asked.

"I've done a little bit of my own research," Gail said. "There is not much on your house but from what I can gather, the child witnessed the murder of her mother. Something like that would damage her soul but that doesn't explain why she's there. She must have died in the house or on the surrounding property and she must feel injustice at that death. Were there some accounts that she hung herself?"

"I have heard that," Jenny said. "But if she committed suicide then why would she haunt the place?"

"It's still possible that she might, because she might feel she was pushed to it. However, it is possible that she was murdered and it was made to look like a suicide. We have seen that before and that would definitely be enough to instigate a haunting."

"Is there anymore I can do?" Jenny asked.

"Hopefully, she has gone and gone for good," Gail said. "However, it is possible that the exorcism only sent her away. In that case she may come back. From what you have told me she's after a family. However, her idea of a family does not involve the father. Your husband would be in danger and from what you've told me, so would Abby. I believe she has bonded with your daughter and the idea of a friend for all eternity will draw her back to you. Your first line of defense is not to invite her in. She has been driven from the house, if you do not invite her back then she cannot enter."

"Thank you," Jenny said. "If she gets back in is there anything we can do?"

"You have to drive her out again but this time it will be harder. What you would really need would be for Abby to tell her to leave as well as the exorcism. Understand, that would be difficult and traumatic for your daughter and if at all possible, you do not want it to come to that. Remember to call us if you need help and if we can we will be there."

After Jenny had finished the call she sat at the kitchen table for some time. The thought of asking Abby to stand up to Victoria turned her stomach and once more she felt sick. How could she do that to her baby?

The house suddenly felt colder and less friendly. Of course, this was a worst-case scenario. They had to hope that Victoria was gone and that she was never coming back. Yet, as Jenny left the kitchen and went back to her painting she felt the hairs prickle on the back of her neck. It was as if someone was watching her.

Chapter Twenty

Jenny couldn't shake the feeling that she was being watched, that something was there, and yet no one else in the house could feel it. The stains had gone from both of the carpets and the house felt less oppressive. Yet, she often saw a shadow at the top of the stairs. Next to the balcony, where she had once seen the ghost of Victoria. She was finding it so hard to settle, and to relax, and yet she did not know why.

Today she was supposed to be finishing the last of her paintings. This was the third time she had tried to complete it and every time it turned out distorted. The light was perfect, she could see birds in the sky outside and the sun was clear and bright. So why did she feel chilled? Why was she looking for something that wasn't there? Picking up a brush she mixed some paint and chose a light blue. It was perfect for this sky and she could see it in her mind. The brush hovered over the canvas but she could not bring herself to touch it. So far, she had been in here over an hour and yet the canvas was as blank as when she started.

All she could think about was a way to stop Victoria. Or what would happen when she came back. It was no longer if in her mind, now it was always when. Yet, she had to hide it from Mason. He was angry with her, angry that she had brought them out here and that now she seemed to be destroying it. The funny thing was, both Mason and Abby had forgotten how bad things had gotten before. To them it was just an incident and not a very big one. Their minds seemed to have clouded over what really happened and invented a story that was much less scary. How could she explain to them that they had to be careful? Or should she just leave? The problem was, she didn't know if they would come with her.

Letting out a big long breath she touched the brush to the canvas and started to paint. Letting her arm flow she concentrated on nothing but the sky and soon it began to take shape.

As she leaned over to switch brushes and colors a shadow crossed behind her. Her heart clenched as she saw it skitter across the floor. Then something touched her back. A shriek of fear left her and she jumped up knocking the canvas and the paints to the floor. They scattered before her as she held up her arms in defense.

"Easy, easy there, it's just me," Mason said.

Jenny could see from the look on his face that he was not happy and she wondered if she would be getting another lecture.

Then his face seemed to relax and he smiled and took her hands.

"You need to talk about this," he said. "I know you are still afraid... but we are safe. The spirit has gone and is not coming back. Maybe it's time to live in the here and now, to just forget all about what happened."

Jenny did not know what to say. Inside she wanted to scream at him to get real. That he must understand the danger and be prepared. That they had to be ready. Yet, as she looked at him she knew he would not understand, could not understand, and so she nodded.

"Maybe you're right, maybe I should talk to someone."

Together they picked up the canvas. It was ruined and yet while she held it Jenny had a thought.

"I'm going to go see Luke, the priest.

Maybe I can talk to him, maybe he can help me."

Mason nodded. "If you can't talk to me then it will be better than no one. Do you want me to come with you?"

"No, I'm happy to go alone."

***

Soon, Jenny was in the car and traveling the twisty, narrow roads towards Crick Howell. Though she had no idea what to say to the priest it felt good to be doing something.

Luke brought her into the old-fashioned kitchen and once more made her a cup of tea in the old ladies' china cups that seemed so out of place for such a young man.

"How you doing?" he asked.

Jenny sipped her tea and wondered what to say. Maybe she should just say okay and yet she was here and she needed help.

"I'm frightened it's not over. That this is just a reprieve and that one day she will be back."

"I understand... in some ways I feel the same so I have been doing some research and have made a number of calls. Though at first, I think they considered me a little nutty, eventually I got passed along to the right people. If anything else happens come to me, and if I find anything out I will come to you."

Jenny was filled with relief at the words of the man who felt like a friend. The next 3 quarters of an hour they drank tea and talked about village matters. There was to be an open day soon and he asked if she would help. Jenny agreed and even offered to do a painting to raffle for church funds. It seemed the least she could do, however, she just hoped she would be able to complete the painting in time.

***

When she got back to the house it was almost dark and Mason was cooking dinner. Chicken nuggets and peas for Abby and he had treated them to a couple of sirloin steaks and some sweet potato French fries. It smelt wonderful as she walked in the door and the house seemed so normal and so welcoming. Maybe talking to Luke had helped, maybe she just needed to voice her fears. To be heard, and now she could let it all go.

"The food's nearly ready," Mason said.

"Looks like we're eating in front of the telly along with some DVD about Dalmatians. I'm sure I've only seen it about 300 times so it should be fun." He winked at her as she put her bag down on the counter.

"I'll get the trays." Jenny started to prepare trays for them to eat on and yet she could not help but worry, where was Abby?

"Is Abby about?"

"She's playing with one of her dolls. We better be careful, I keep getting the question, you know... maybe we could have a dog?"

Jenny found herself laughing. It happened every time they saw this film but she had to admit the puppies were very cute.

"Maybe we should," she said before she even realized.

Mason was serving chicken nuggets onto a plate and his mouth fell open.

"Are you serious?"

Jenny didn't know. For one crazy moment she thought that maybe a dog would be protection against Victoria and then she shook her head.

"I don't know, it seemed like a good idea for a second or two."

Mason was laughing as he handed her Abby's tray.

"Can I have ice cream for afters?" Jenny asked as she took the tray through to the living room and found Abby on the floor talking away to... for a moment she froze and then Abby lifted the doll. Letting out her breath, she helped her onto the sofa and then passed her the tray. Had she really thought that Mr. Good Bear was back?

Mason came in with two more trays and they all settled down on the sofa to watch the film.

The steaks were very good. Rare enough to bleed. They were soft and melt-in-the-mouth tasty. Normally, she would have taken the trays away but tonight she couldn't be bothered so once they had finished they just put them on the floor and then curled up together on the sofa. Abby was in between them, her eyes locked on the screen and the hundreds of spotty puppies.

She was leaning forward as the room filled with shadows. Jenny got up and put on the lights. It was unusual. Normally, they would watch the film in the dark and she saw Mason's eyes question but he didn't say anything. Abby was engrossed as the older dogs started the twilight bark. She loved that bit and would not move for anything.

The film got to the part where the puppies had been found and suddenly the lights went off and the telly died.

Jenny felt her breath catch in her throat and her heart was pounding against her chest. It was happening. She was here! Though she knew she should do something she could not move.

"I'll go grab a torch," Mason said so matter-of-factly it was obvious that he thought it nothing more than a power cut.

Mason stood but before Jenny could move she felt Abby stand from in between them.

Gradually, Jenny's eyes were adjusting to the dark. Mason had gone and she watched Abby walking towards the patio doors. Did she see a shape outside?

As Jenny opened her mouth to scream, no, she watched the shape coalesce and form. It was Victoria.

"Abby, come back here," she screamed but it was too late.

"Victoria wants to come in," Abby said.

Jenny was moving now and shouting but it was too late. Before she could cross the room to stop her Abby opened the patio door. "Come in," she said and stood to one side.

As soon as Victoria came inside she seemed to gain in strength and though she was still translucent Jenny could see her face. It bore a smile but it wasn't friendly. In fact, it spoke of malice and victory. The spirit was like a shadow on the world, like a shape that had been superimposed badly and was faint but there. Yet, she was real enough to hurt them, of that Jenny was sure,

"You are not welcome here," Jenny shouted.

Victoria spun around to face her and let out a shriek of anger. Raising her arm she swiped it from left to right.

As Jenny watched, Abby was flung across the room and hit the wall with a terrible thud. Jenny ran to her daughter and took her in her arms.

"Are you hurt?"

Abby shook her head but there were tears in her eyes.

"I don't understand," Abby said. "She is my friend."

"You have to tell her to leave, you have to tell her you don't want her here anymore," Jenny whispered the word so only Abby could hear them but she could see her daughter was afraid and was shaking her head.

Jenny put herself in between Abby and Victoria and stood to face her. At the same time Mason ran back into the room with a torch. The beam sliced through the darkness and where it intersected with Victoria it seemed to cut her in two. It was as if she was a creature of the dark and where the light touched her she was banished. Could they use this? Somehow, Jenny doubted they could and yet still it felt positive.

Once more, Victoria shrieked in anger and Mason was sent flying across the room. He hit the wall and fell to the floor.

"What do you want?" Jenny screamed.

"I want you as my family. I want you as my mother, Abby as my sister, and the child as my brother. I want this for all time and what I want I always get. Come with me now and I will let Daddy leave."

"We are here as your family," Jenny said. "Only there are three of us. Mason is part of our family and you can be too but not like this."

"He has to go," Victoria said and she clenched her fists and turned towards him.

Jenny wondered if maybe she was afraid of Mason, if perhaps he was a threat to her. If that was the case then she needed to keep him here, needed to give him time to recover and to do whatever Victoria was afraid of. Her own fear was like a beast inside of her. The fear for Abby, who was crying in the corner. The fear for Mason, the fear of what Victoria would do to him, and the fear of this evil creature in front of her. Fear that she might not be able to get rid of her. Yet, she remembered her talk with Gail and she knew that fear would feed the spirit. So she took a deep breath and swallowed down her fear. Closing her eyes for just a second she centered herself and when she opened them she was strong as she looked back at Victoria.

Did she see the spirit shimmer?

Slowly, she was walking around trying to get in front of Mason, to try and see if she could help him and all the time she was talking slowly and quietly to Victoria.

"What is it you want from a family? Is it talking, company, someone to teach you lessons? If you let me know what you want then we can help you." Gradually, as she talked, she worked her way around towards Mason.

"I want you and Abby and I want him gone." As Victoria said the words she circled her hands and the room seemed to fill with the wind.

Jenny could feel it building, could feel the pressure, she knew something was about to happen. What should she do? There seemed no answer, seemed no way to help. It was down to Abby, Abby had to tell her to leave and yet she was too afraid. It was too much to ask such a little girl.

Jenny was moving away from Mason now to try and get to Abby. It was a hard decision but it was the only one she could make.

The temperature in the room dropped and she watched her breath mist before her and somehow she knew that something was going to happen and it would be soon.

Victoria pulled her arms back and then swept them forward, as she did the trays, plates, and cutlery from the floor were sent like weapons towards Mason. He was picked up by the wind and slammed into the wall and all of the objects hit him one by one. At first a plate, and then a tray. Jenny was screaming as she watched the assault rain down on him. The cutlery smashed against him but one steak knife turned. Jenny let out a scream as she watched it puncture his chest. Blood streamed from the wound and he was slammed back once more and then the wind was gone and he dropped to the floor.

"No, Mason. No," Jenny screamed as she saw him lying face down just inside the door. A pool of blood was spreading out from beneath him and he was deadly still.

Chapter Twenty-One

Victoria let out a shrill and yet delighted laugh and seemed to float towards them.

Jenny wanted to run to Mason, wanted to check on him, to call an ambulance and to get them out of there and yet all she could do was stand in front of Abby. She tried to whisper to Abby to tell her to send Victoria away, to tell her to leave, but she couldn't. Even if she did, Victoria would never hear it over the child's own tears.

As she watched, the spirit drifted closer and the air seemed to be sucked out of the room and replaced with ice. Jenny felt each breath was painful. Like splinters in her lungs and she wanted to hug Abby but she would not go behind her. She would face this and stop this, she just didn't know how.

"Now we can be together," Victoria said as she floated even closer.

"Not like this," Jenny managed, she knew she had to stay calm to stay rational to try and fight this creature any way she could. She looked up and could see something in Victoria's hand.

It was a noose.

Bit by bit Victoria got closer and bit by bit they backed away. Abby was hanging onto her waist and was staying with her. It was all she could do for her at the moment.

The spirit was herding them back towards Mason, towards the door. Jenny didn't really know why but she knew it had something to do with the stains, the balcony. That was the place where she had seen Victoria the most. Was that where they were going?

"You just have to use this," Victoria said shaking the noose before them. "Then we can all be together."

"Not like this," Jenny shouted. "You will never get us like this."

"We will be together, forever." Victoria advanced, the noose held out before her like some form of a gift. Maybe that was what she thought it was!

The pressure in the room grew even stronger. Jenny could feel her chest being crushed. Tears came to her eyes as she bit down to try and control the pain. Was this happening to Abby? How she hoped it wasn't. How she hoped the spirit could hone her power and hurt just one of them.

Little by little they backed through the darkness until they were level with Mason. As she slid her foot back the floor was slick and she let out a gasp as they walked through his blood.

"Oh no, oh no, Mason." Jenny wanted to drop to the floor, to see how he was and yet she couldn't. For if she did then it would expose Abby. So, she slid her feet backward through the blood straining her eyes for any sign that Mason was still alive.

Victoria was coming closer and each time she did the pressure increased so Jenny had no choice but to back away. Abby was shaking and weeping silently now as she clutched to her waist.

Once in the hallway Jenny could see the keys in the front door. It was the key to the house and the key to the car. Would she be fast enough? Could she get out of here and get Abby away? If she did would Victoria follow them or would she kill Mason? The problem was, Jenny thought he was already dead and that if they didn't at least try, that they would be dead soon too.

Turning, she scooped Abby into her arms and ran for the door. She pushed so hard it felt as if she was falling forward and with each step the pressure eased. Breathing became easier and she adjusted Abby in her arms to free up her right hand. It was so close, she reached out to grab for the key. Could almost feel it in her fingers and relief flooded through her, they had made it. Only her hand missed and she felt her feet leave the floor. She was spun around so quickly that she felt sick and then slammed into the wall next to the kitchen door. The wind was knocked from her and her head felt as if it had been crushed. Somewhere along the line she had dropped Abby. Panic rose inside her as she scoured the darkness, desperate to see her child.

Though it was still very dark her eyes were adjusting to the gloom. Shapes were coming into focus and there was movement before her. Try as she might Jenny could not move. The more she strained the more her lungs ached and the stronger the pressure grew. Only she had to move, she had to find Abby. Then she saw her. It was the scene that she had seen many times. Abby was walking across the magnificent hallway her right arm held out as if she was holding a hand. Only this time she was. Victoria stood beside her holding that confounded bear. The blood stain was clearly visible in the dark. It glistened as if catching all the light.

Taking Abby by the hand, Victoria walked past Jenny and on towards the kitchen door.

"Abby, don't go with her, baby. Tell her to get out of here." The pressure inside Jenny's lungs grew until she was gasping for breath.

They walked on by, Abby gave her a glance and a weak smile but she did not stop.

Jenny knew that things were coming to a head. That if she did not act soon that it would be too late and yet, what could she do?

Victoria had taken Abby to the stain on the carpet. The stain that was back and that somehow represented her death. Hung above it was the noose and suddenly Jenny understood. Using every ounce of strength she had she fought against the force holding her. The spirit was going to kill her child and if she did not get free it would happen right here and now before her very eyes.

"Tell her to go, Abby. You have to tell it to go." The effort to speak was like drowning. Each word took her precious breath and filled her lungs with pressure and yet she would not stop.

"I don't want to do this," Abby said, her voice so faint it was hardly audible in the big hall.

"You must." Victoria shoved the noose towards her. "I am so lonely and you are my friend. This means we can be together, forever."

"What about my mummy?"

As Jenny watched, she saw the spirit lean down and whisper something in Abby's ear and the noose was gone.

Jenny let out a breath, had it worked, was it over? Then she saw Victoria pointing upward and they looked up. On the balcony was a man and Victoria. She was dressed in a white nightdress that was covered in blood and she was crying and so very young. The man took a noose and put it around her neck and then he lifted her onto the balcony. Jenny did not want to watch, did not want Abby to watch.

"Close your eyes, baby," she called just as the man pushed Victoria from the balcony.

There was the sound of her falling, it was like a huge set of wings that whooshed through the air. For a moment, she thought of angels. Only this was no miracle, the man was a vulture and it was the wings of death she could hear. Then the rope snapped her body to a halt and the sound of her neck breaking was like a gunshot in the dark airless house. Victoria was left dangling there, her eyes closed, her head down and her tongue hanging loose. Her bladder and bowels opened and pooled onto the carpet.

Jenny felt a rush of sorrow for the child. She had not deserved this and she vowed to help her if they got out of here but that was their first priority.

The vision was gone and Victoria was shaking Abby and pushing the rope towards her. As she watched, Abby's eyes opened wide and she shrank back shaking her head.

"Tell her to leave," Jenny shouted and Abby looked towards her.

"Tell it to leave, baby, tell it to go for your daddy and for me, please, just tell it to go." Jenny wanted to say more but the effort was too much. There was nothing left in her lungs except pain. The urge to breathe was automatic and her body gasped and choked trying to suck in air.

"Just put your head in here and you will soon be free," Victoria said as she pulled the noose lower and held it in front of Abby's neck.

"What about Mummy and Daddy?" Abby was crying, big brown eyes peered through long black hair the color of raven's wings. Silent tears ran down her face as she pleaded for help.

Would it ever come?

First, she looked at Jenny and then towards the doorway where her father lay motionless.

"If we all do this then we can all be together soon." Victoria moved the noose closer.

"Even Daddy?"

Victoria didn't answer but the room cooled once more and Jenny could sense her anger.

A scraping sound from the entrance to the ballroom pulled all eyes towards it.

Jenny could not believe it, as she saw Mason's arm reach out. There was something in it but she could not quite make it out. His fingers moved and picked up the object.

"Mason!" Jenny managed but it left her gasping for breath.

Then the object dropped from his hand and clattered across the floor and he was motionless once more.

Despite the fact that she was held against the wall Jenny felt her knees collapse.

Mason was dead, she was sure of it, and soon Abby and she would follow. In a last desperate bid, she sucked in as much air as she could, ready to talk to Abby one more time.

The noose was now around Abby's neck and as Jenny watched it was drawn tight. Then from behind her she heard the priest's voice. Spinning around, she expected to see Luke stood in the doorway but he was not there. However, the slight glow from the mobile screen told her what Mason had done. She remembered back to finding his mobile phone in her pocket after the first exorcism. Mason had slipped it there before they went back into the house. Jenny never asked him why or what he was doing but now she understood. Mason had recorded the exorcism, he would save them.

"Our Father, who art in heaven, hallowed be Thy name. Thy kingdom come," Luke's voice was clear over the phone even if a little tinny.

Victoria shrieked in anger and the phone was sent spinning across the floor. Jenny prayed that it would not be harmed. It hit the skirting board and bounced back but the exorcism kept playing. Mason was so still that she had to bite back a scream of anguish. Was he dead?

"Thy will be done on earth as it is in

heaven. Give us this day our daily bread and forgive us our trespasses as we forgive those who trespass against us."

"Abby, tell her to leave," Jenny shouted.

"I don't want to do this," Abby said, her voice shallow and weak.

"And lead us not into temptation, but deliver us from evil. Amen."

For a moment the noose tightened and Abby was lifted from her feet. The sound of her struggling for breath tore at Jenny's heart and she struggled even harder.

"Tell it to leave, baby, just tell it to leave."

"Visit this place, O Lord, we pray, and drive far from it the snares of the enemy," the exorcism continued on the phone.

"Get away from her," Jenny screamed and suddenly she was free and racing across the hallway.

"May your holy angels dwell with us and guard us in peace."

She grabbed hold of Abby's ankles and lifted her up. Instantly, the child could breathe more easily and she could see that Victoria was no longer so sure.

"Tell her to leave, Abby," Jenny shouted as she reached up and freed the nose from her neck.

"I don't want to play anymore," Abby said as Jenny hugged her close. She was eye to eye with Victoria and could see the anger in the spirit but she could also see through her. Victoria was no longer solid but was translucent and fading.

"Get out of here, you are not welcome," she shouted and the spirit faded even more. The air was easing and the temperature was rising.

"And may your blessing be always upon us; through Jesus Christ our Lord. Amen," the phone played on.

Victoria faded away to nothing.

Tears were streaming down Jenny's face as she hugged Abby to her. Then she ran to the phone and called for an ambulance.

Chapter Twenty-Two

Long black hair looked stark against the bleached white of the pillow. Abby's eyes were closed and her face relaxed. It was a sight that filled Jenny with hope and joy. Despite what she had been through, Abby was sleeping peacefully. The only injuries the hospital could find were a rope burn around her neck and a few cuts and bruises. All in all, she had gotten off very lightly.

While they tended to her daughter, Jenny had refused treatment for herself. There was a scrape on her head, cuts and bruises on her arms and back but nothing that she couldn't cope with. She let her eyes drift around the gray walls to the blue curtain surrounding the bed. It was late now, past midnight, and it all seemed so peaceful and yet Jenny couldn't relax. Mason was out of surgery but she didn't know how bad his injury was. Her hands twisted in her lap as she tried to sit still but it was impossible. Taking a last long look at Abby she got up and slipped out from behind the curtain. There were five other beds in the room and each of the occupants was sleeping. Being careful to make as little noise as possible Jenny crept from the ward.

The corridors were all empty. Painted a stark grey with black and red lines traced along the floor. Jenny knew to follow the red line down to the intensive care unit where she could check once more on Mason.

As she pushed through the doors the nurse looked up, a weary smile crossed her face and she nodded at Jenny to come over.

"Is there any news?" Jenny asked.

"It's good news. He's out of surgery, the injury was not as bad as we first thought. The main problem was blood loss and a blow to the head. We think the reason he was unconscious was the blow had caused a concussion. The knife wound itself missed all of the major organs and will heal without any lasting effects. The head wound will heal also but he needs to be observed for the next 48 hours. The main thing he will need is plenty of fluids and rest. They will be keeping him on a drip to keep him hydrated and to make sure that his brain does not swell. Once he has come around the doctor doesn't want him to be left alone for the next 10 hours. So, they will be keeping him here under observation for just a couple of days."

Jenny felt a rush of relief so strong that it almost dropped her to her knees.

"Thank you, thank you so much. Can I see him?"

"He's just coming out of recovery now and I can show you through in a moment or two. It will be another half an hour or so before he wakes but there is no problem with you sitting with him. How is your daughter?"

Jenny couldn't stop a smile from spreading across her face.

"She's doing fine, thank you. In fact, she's fast asleep and doesn't remember a thing." As soon as she had said it Jenny wished she hadn't. So far, she hadn't given the hospital any explanation of what had happened and she knew that conversation was coming. Luckily, the nurse just smiled and then showed her through to Mason's bedside.

He was sleeping peacefully and, despite a large bruise and gash on his head, he looked as good as new. Jenny pulled up a chair next to him and took his hand in hers. Gently, she lay her head on his hand and tried to get some sleep. Only her mind wouldn't stop working. Was this over? Was it safe to go back to the house, would it ever be safe?

Though she tried to rest, it was

impossible and she found herself looking down at her clothes. They were dirty and torn and suddenly, she wanted to shower and change. Maybe she should go home... home, was it their home yet? Maybe she should go back to the house and pick up a change of clothing for all of them. Surely, it was safe? Abby had told Victoria to leave and the spirit had gone. That had to mean it was over.

Jenny tried to rest for another 15 minutes but she just couldn't sit still. In the end, she left a message with the nurse and drove back to the house.

She pulled the car up into the driveway and noticed the door was open and the lights were on. She couldn't remember whether they had left the door open when the ambulance came. Maybe she had. At the time, she certainly had other things on her mind. One thing she did know was the lights hadn't been on for the power was still out when they left. It must be a good sign that there was power now! Perhaps it confirmed that the spirit had finally gone. Jenny was too tired to think about it too much and so she shook her head and pushed the thought away.

Getting out of the car she felt a chill wind. For a second, she tensed and then laughed... it was simply natural, a breeze. As she looked up at the house she felt her breath catch. It was beautiful, the twin turrets, the large windows. It looked inviting and like everything she had always dreamed of. For a few seconds, she just stared at the house trying to feel if Victoria was still there. Concentrating all her senses, she searched for anything that was wrong... there was nothing that she could find. It seemed she had a choice. She could stand here, she could turn around and leave, or she could go in and have a shower. In the end her aching muscles and a feeling of grime down her back won her over.

As she entered the house she kept her senses on full alert. Scanning the rooms for any sign of darkness or chill but there was nothing. Quickly, she made her way to the master bedroom and waited for the sense of despair, of gloom to come over her but it never happened. Carefully, she stepped around the stain on the carpet. It was hard to tell if it was any worse. The damn thing was such a part of the room now and seemed to change on a daily basis that she could not keep it straight in her head. Skirting around it, she headed for the shower.

Stripping off, she stepped into the stream of hot water and felt immediately relaxed. Leaning against the wall she let the water pound on to her shoulders and back and found that tears were running from her eyes as the water ran over her face. They had survived, they had beaten it and the relief was more than she could take.

Little by little the water brought her back to herself. It eased the aching muscles, washed away the grime, and made her feel more human again. At last she turned off the water and stepped from the shower. Grabbing a big fluffy bath sheet she wrapped it around herself and sat on the bed. For some reason she had sat with her feet almost touching the stain. Instead of filling her with disgust it filled her with sadness and once again she found tears in her eyes. What had Victoria seen? What had she gone through? The feeling of sadness was overwhelming and the more she thought about it the sorrier she felt for the child. At the end of the day she was a victim as much as they were, probably even more so.

What if it had been her child?

If something so traumatic had happened to Abby, would she want her to be simply banished? Her thoughts kept going back to the little room in the attic and the lonely grave in the woods and it broke her heart. Something had to be done and now that her family was safe she felt able to do it. Quickly, she dried herself and pulled on some jeans and a sweatshirt. If Victoria was still here she had to try and help. It made sense. Not only to help the poor desperate spirit but to save her family, the only problem was she didn't know how to help.

Quickly, she found her tablet and sent

an email to Gail Parker telling her exactly what had happened and what she planned to do. Though she knew that Gail and her ghost hunting partner, Jesse, were currently in Bulgaria, and there was probably nothing they could do to help, it still felt good to send off a message.

Just half a minute later the tablet pinged a notification of a reply.

Don't do anything. We will leave tomorrow and be with you as soon as possible. Keep away from the house and keep safe.

Regards,

Gail.

Jenny stared at the message for a long time. Her hand hovered over the screen. Though she knew it was good advice and that she should follow it she felt she could not leave the house. The sadness was more than she could bear. What mother could leave a child in such pain? Victoria was not evil but simply a lonely lost soul and she needed her help. What sort of decent human being would she be if she walked away from this?

Face down, she dropped the tablet on the bed and, picking up a battery lantern, she strolled out of the room. Turning right she headed for the attic. Somehow, she knew that was where Victoria wanted her and she hoped that going there would help the child heal.

Chapter Twenty-Three

Jenny felt drawn towards the attic. It was as if she would find answers there. Without hesitation, she climbed the first seven steps, turned the corner, and climbed the next seven. The door was open. For just a second she hesitated. Last time she was here she distinctly remembered closing it and sliding the bolt across to keep it locked. Who had opened it?

Reaching up she pulled the cord and a faint yellow light appeared in the distance. It was like a beacon drawing her onward and she stepped into the attic and followed the dusty path between the boxes. There were small footsteps leading the way. Seeing them raised the hairs on the back of her neck. They could only belong to a child and she felt the need to hurry. It was as if she was being pulled towards an answer. Gradually, she weaved through the boxes towards the light. It shone down on the trunk. The one where she had found the journal and read about the awful things that had happened to Victoria. When she reached it, the trunk was open and three of the dolls stood up and stared at her. Their eyes seemed to follow her as she knelt before the trunk.

The journal was gone.

That didn't surprise her, she knew it would be. To her left she heard the sound of giggling. It was the sound of a child playing hide and seek. One that wanted to be quiet but could not quite stop her own exuberance, and yet there was something more to the sound. Something sinister that scraped across the nerves like the tapping of something unseen on a dark and lonely night.

Jenny knew she had to follow the sound and so she turned and walked around the boxes and towards the sad little room where Victoria had spent much of her time. Something tickled across her face and her hands scrabbled out desperate to find it.

It was just a cobweb! Nothing to fear and yet her heart was pounding so fast it felt as if it would burst at any moment. Still, she kept walking and there before her was the room made out of boxes. Once more it reminded her of an igloo. The little tunnel in the bottom designed for Victoria to crawl through. She looked down at the floor and could see that the dust had been disturbed. Someone had been in here recently, but who?

Of course, that was obvious. Victoria was here and she was waiting for her.

Logically, Jenny wanted to turn and run from the house and yet she felt drawn towards that dark tunnel. As she looked towards the opening a faint glow flickered from beneath the boxes. Perhaps this time the candle was already lit. Remembering the lantern in her hand, she switched it on and knelt down. It would be a tight squeeze for her to get under the boxes and into the room but it was possible. She pushed the lantern into the gap and tried to look past it, it was impossible. From her last visit she remembered a blanket, a doll, a journal, and a candle stub.

Pushing the lantern before her she crawled into the opening. Panic raged inside of her as the boxes closed in on either side and for a moment she was trapped. The urge to thrash and kick and punch her way out of there was overwhelming. However, if she did that then the boxes would come tumbling down and Victoria might be hurt. For a moment, her mind wanted to laugh.

The ghost couldn't be hurt, it was a ghost!

However, her heart knew this was not true. Victoria could be hurt, she was hurt, and that was the reason for the trouble. As a frightened and damaged child she was lashing out at them. Jenny must do whatever she could to help her. She just hoped that she would be able to walk away afterward and stay with her own family.

***

Slowly, Mason came around. It was dark but not totally so and he scanned the room looking for Jenny, for Abby, and for any sign of danger. There was a deep ache in his skull and he reached up to his head. Carefully, he searched for the injury and when his hand touched a dressing he pulled it away confused.

Where was he?

Sitting up he felt a wave of nausea and had to pull himself backward and lean against what he thought was the wall. Only, it wasn't the wall, he was in a bed. That must mean he was safe, that his family was safe. Gradually his eyes accustomed to the dark and he worked out he was in a hospital. Where were Jenny and Abby?

Swallowing, he tried to call out but his throat was too dry and the words came out as nothing more than a croak. Though he knew he should rest he couldn't. What if his family were still in danger? Slowly, he swung his legs over the side of the bed and tried to stand. Something caught on his arm and pulled him back and then a wave of nausea sent him crashing back onto the bed.

"Oh, no you don't, get back in that bed," a young nurse said as she arrived at his bedside.

Mason tried to talk again but once more he couldn't. The nurse nodded and handed him a glass of water. She pressed a button and raised the back of the bed so that he was sitting up and able to drink. Gratefully, he took a few swallows and handed the glass back.

"My family?" he asked.

"They are fine. Your daughter is in the children's ward and your wife went home for a shower and some fresh clothing. You just need to rest and you'll be fine in a day or two."

Mason nodded and yet the thought of Jenny back at the house scared him more than he could say. Would she be safe?

As the nurse wandered off he checked himself over. What had stopped his arm was an IV. It was connected to a bag of fluid. The rest of him seemed okay. Just a few cuts and bruises but nothing too much. He knew he had to get up and to go check on Jenny and yet he needed to stop his head spinning. Closing his eyes he relaxed back against the bed for just a moment. Just to gain his strength and yet before he could think of what he had to do, he fell back into a deep sleep.

***

The darkness closed in around Jenny as she struggled to crawl between the boxes. There was a light up ahead. It was a beacon, safety, if only she could get to it and yet she was frozen. Hunkered down and trying to keep small. Maybe if she stayed still she would be safe. Then she thought of Abby and Mason. Gritting her teeth, she forced her body to move. First one hand and then the other, she made her way towards the light and out of the darkness. The closer she got the faster she was moving. It was as if the devil was chasing her.

Panting so hard she was almost hyperventilating, she shot from between the boxes and into the room. Standing up she took in a few deep breaths and managed to calm herself. Gradually, her eyes were becoming accustomed to the gloom. The room was lit by nothing more than the tiny candle. She could see the lantern; it had been knocked against the far wall of boxes and turned off. However, it was light enough to see and she didn't need it for now.

Sat`in front of her holding Mr. Good Bear was Victoria. Her legs were crossed beneath her on a blanket and the candle was to one side. It was so close to the blanket that Jenny felt herself gasp. The thought of that naked flame in amongst all of this paper and the blanket and this little girl scared the very life out of her. How she wanted to extinguish it and yet she was too afraid.

Victoria was staring, her hands were gripping the arms of the bear so tightly that her knuckles were white. She was wearing the white nightgown, the splashes of blood on it had faded to brown. Jenny knew she had to do something and yet she didn't know what. The feeling of sadness, of desperation was so strong that she wanted to give up. Slowly, she lowered herself to the floor and sat in front of Victoria. For a moment, she just sat and stared at the child, giving her a slight smile and trying to offer comfort. As she watched, Victoria began to relax and she held out her hands. It made Jenny nervous and yet she felt compelled to do the same. Slowly, she reached out and took Victoria's hands. They were cold and insubstantial. As she held them they seemed to harden beneath her fingers. Despair fell over her like a cold mist. It brought with it a loss of hope and she felt the fight to go on evaporating from her. Maybe she should just stay here with Victoria for all time.

Caroline Clark

Chapter Twenty-Four

Mason gradually came awake once more. As his eyes opened, at first, he struggled to focus. The room was just a blur. Raising his arm, he rubbed at them until his vision cleared. It was daylight. Where was Jenny?

Though his mind was fuzzy he remembered the terrors of the night before and sat up a little too quickly. A wave of nausea pushed him back to the bed and he pulled in a few deep breaths.

Where was Jenny? If she had just gone back to the house for a shower and some clothes then surely she would be back by now. Maybe she had just gone for coffee and would be back any minute. Hoping that was the case he reached out for the glass and took another drink of water. It was cool and refreshing as it slid down his throat and it made him feel instantly stronger.

His fingers tapped on the bed as the

seconds slipped into minutes and Jenny did not come back. Where was she? Has something happened? The more he thought about it the more afraid he became and yet his mind could not remember why he was afraid. It was something to do with the house and a girl but he could not remember what.

Maybe if he lay just a little bit longer then the memories would come back. Closing his eyes he tried to think and yet he was overwhelmed with fear for Jenny. Somehow, he knew he had to go, that he had to help her and that if he stayed here too long it would be too late.

There was no one around and he could see his clothes on a chair in the corner. The IV was still attached to his arm. Cautiously, he peeled back the tape that held the needle and then, gritting his teeth, he pulled the needle free. A bright spot of blood appeared in the spot where the needle had been. Tearing off a bit of the tape he stuck it over the hole and hoped for the best.

The sense of urgency was growing and he threw back the thin blanket and swung his legs over the side of the bed.

Gingerly, he tested to see if they would hold his weight. Though he felt a touch of nausea he didn't fall and he managed to stumble to the chair. Taking the clothes off the chair he sat down and dressed. It was a difficult and laborious process that left his head spinning and his stomach churning and yet he managed it, eventually.

Now all he had to do was get out of the hospital without being seen. Luckily, he had his wallet on him. It would be easy enough to get a taxi back to the house. What happened after that would not be as easy.

***

In reality, Jenny knew that she was sat on the floor in the box room of the attic holding the hands of the ghost and yet in her mind she was playing a ring of roses in the sunshine with her best friend. They were dancing around and singing and laughing and it was wonderful and fun.

"Stay with me forever," Victoria whispered in her ear as she passed.

Jenny spun around dancing and laughing. She wanted to say yes and yet there was something nagging at the back of her mind. It was another little girl, one with dark black hair and pale blue eyes. She tried to see the face and remember the child's name and yet she could not. All she saw was the little blonde girl before her, her ringlets bouncing as she jumped and her bright smile that looked so happy.

Round and round and round they go. Singing and laughing.

"Ring a Ring a roses, a pocket full of posies, atishoo atishoo, we all fall down."

Jenny dropped to her knees on the floor as did Victoria. As she felt the earth on her knees something happened. It wasn't, it was the hard wooden floor of the attic and for a moment it brought her back to reality. Abby's face appeared before her and her child was frightened. She was holding the hand of a man and at first Jenny did not know who he was. Then her mind seemed to clear and she knew it was Mason. How could she forget him, how could she forget Abby? Suddenly, she knew she had to get out of here and yet she did not have the strength or the energy and maybe she would have just one more dance and then she could think about being serious. Not now though, now she wanted to have fun and to play.

***

When Mason got back to the house he found that the priest was waiting for him and the front door was open.

"Have you been inside?" Mason asked, his voice a little confrontational. He wasn't sure if he meant that the priest had left the door open or if he was angry because he hadn't been in and checked on Jenny. It was difficult, his mind would still not fully remember what had happened the night before.

"Good morning, Mr. Evans," Luke said. "You look hurt but I believe that time is short and so I will get straight to the point. I haven't been inside the house and refused to do so. Has something else happened?"

Mason ran a hand through his thick dark hair and across the stubble of his chin as he tried to work out what to say.

"It was last night, I don't remember what happened, but I woke up in the hospital. I had been stabbed and knocked unconscious. Abby is in hospital too but it is just cuts and bruises. Jenny came home last night to have a shower and get some more clothes." Suddenly Mason was frightened. Something had happened to Jenny and he was stood here talking. He had to get into the house and to save her. Turning from the priest he started to run towards the door. A hand grabbed hold of his arm and pulled him up short.

"We can help her more if we put the spirit to rest," Luke said.

Mason had been spun around and was looking into the man's eyes. The urge to punch him was strong. To shake off his hand and to run into the house and save Jenny. Yet the memories from last night, though sketchy, told him that his chances of success were slim. A wave of nausea washed over him. Had he really just contemplated punching a priest? Shaking his head he relaxed.

"I'm sorry, I'm just so scared of what may have happened to her."

"I understand and that is why I am here. I've been doing some research, much of it you already know. Victoria was found hanging from the balcony, her father claimed she committed suicide and in his grief blamed his wife and killed her. Or at least, that is his story. There is another report that the father killed the wife and then hung the child. Throwing her body from the balcony. Either way, at the time the suicide was believed. As the child had taken her own life she was not allowed to be buried in the churchyard. I have been speaking to some experts and they believe that if we find her body and move it to consecrated ground and then bless and salt her bones that this will be over. She will be laid to rest. The problem is I have no idea where she is buried and it could be anywhere."

Mason let out a big breath of relief.

"I know where she is buried," he said. "We found the grave in the trees, Abby found the grave in the woodland. She believes that Victoria led her to it, wanted her to join her there."

"We have to hurry," Luke said. "I believe the spirit is looking for somebody, anybody to keep her company. She will try to persuade your wife to join her. We must move her before she can do that."

Mason nodded and turned to run towards the woods. He didn't bother looking back to see if the priest was following him but grabbed a shovel from behind the house and ran as fast as he could. As he entered the woods the trees seemed to be whipped into a frenzy by the wind. The branches lashed out at him, slashing at his face and knocking into his shoulders. It didn't stop him and barely slowed him down as he raced along the path towards the sad little grave all alone in the woods.

They came out into the clearing and for a second, he saw Victoria. Her arms were crossed before her, her head was held back and the look on her face was defiant. Luke came up behind him and he heard him let out a gasp.

"You can see her?" Mason asked.

"Yes, I see her. Now hurry."

Luke walked past the spirit and towards the little grave and started to dig. Mason expected Victoria to attack him but then he heard Jenny, she was singing. It was a nursery rhyme about little Miss Moffat. She was calling Victoria back to share tea with her.

"Keep her busy, my love," Mason whispered. "But stay with me, please don't go. Just hold on, Jenny, for we are working on this. Just hold on a little longer."

As he watched Victoria faded and then she was gone.

The priest was on his knees digging at the grave. Mason got down to join him and he just hoped that this was the right call. That they would be in time to save Jenny.

Chapter Twenty-Five

Jenny was sat on the floor in the small room pretending to serve tea. In her mind's eye she was wearing a pretty pink dress and in front of her was a table with two teacups and saucers. There was also a jug of milk and a dish with sugar cubes and a pair of silver tongs. Each of the saucers also had a silver spoon.

Smiling across at Victoria she poured the pretend teapot and heard the dark liquid dribble into the pretend cups. It was such fun and she loved to see the smile on her friend's face. Once both cups were filled she put down the teapot and picked up the tongs.

"How many sugars? I like three."

Quickly, she picked up a pretend cube and watched it splash into the pretend tea. Victoria's smile had slipped and her own hand began to shake as she lifted another pretend cube and then another. Only her friend was angry now and she didn't know why. The pale cheeks had turned red, her dark brows had narrowed beneath the bounce of her blonde ringlets.

"You should have done mine first," Victoria snapped. "I'm the guest. I should have been first. If you don't want to stay with me I will bring someone else and they will have to stay forever."

Jenny knew the words were a threat and inside, she was terrified and yet she did not understand why. For some reason, she knew that it had to be her who played with Victoria, forever, but she could not understand why. Her hand was shaking now and she was unsure what to do. If she upset the girl too much then maybe she would be sent away. Who would replace her? The question nagged at the back of Jenny's mind and she wanted to find the answer. Somehow, she knew it was important and yet she was so tired. Whenever she tried to escape from the game she felt so tired and so lethargic that she just wanted to run back to it.

Then Victoria smiled and everything was okay again.

"I want six cubes of sugar," Victoria said. "You must do them for me and don't forget to stir!"

Once more, Jenny found her hand was shaking but she put on the best smile she could and picked up a sugar lump. The tongs were slippery in her hand and she was so afraid that she would drop it but she managed to get it to the tea and let it drop with a small splash. She repeated the task five more times and with each one she gained confidence for she could see her friend starting to smile. This was how it was meant to be, it was fun and this was what would happen for the rest of her days. As she had that thought she felt afraid. There was something else she should be doing and yet she couldn't remember what it was.

"I'm not sure if I should be here," she said before she could stop the words.

The air in the room cooled and she rubbed her arms to keep warm. Victoria's face was angry again and she knew she had said the wrong thing.

"Maybe I should go and find Abby," Victoria said, and she turned and began to fade.

Jenny remembered, Abby was her daughter and she had to keep her safe. Somehow, she had to keep Victoria here until she could find out a way to get rid of her. Only how could she do that?

"Don't go before you've had your tea, it will go cold." Quickly she picked up her own pretend cup and took a pretend drink.

"Mmmmm, this is such good tea. I can get out the biscuits and cakes if you want?"

Victoria turned and sat back down.

"I like bourbons, and Victoria sponge cake," she said as she picked up a cup.

Feeling suddenly strange, as if she was in a dream world, Jenny picked up a pretend tin and opened it, then she got a pretend plate and piled on some pretend biscuits. What had just a few minutes ago been really fun was now the most frightening thing she had ever done. She was starting to remember, to understand what was going on. That she had to keep this child here. Had to keep it away from her own baby, how was she going to do that for any length of time?"

Victoria reached out and picked up a biscuit.

"I don't think you can have any," Victoria said, her voice thick with spite. "You've been having mean thoughts and until you're a good girl you can't have anything else to eat."

Just as she said that the candle blew out and the small room was plunged into darkness.

***

Luke and Mason were digging as fast as

they could but the ground was hard and tree roots crisscrossed through it making it a slow and laborious process. Once more they came to a thick root blocking their path.

"Stand up," Mason said.

As soon as the priest had done so he took the spade he was holding and slammed it down as hard as he could on the root. The spade stopped so quickly that the force bounced back up the handle and into his shoulder. The pain through his wound was incredible and for a moment the world went black. Mason knew he was swaying and he started to fall. In a last desperate effort he put out an arm to save himself but then there was nothing but blackness.

Mason woke in a world of pain looking up at the face of the priest. It was lined with worry and maybe a little fear.

"Are you okay?" Luke asked.

"What happened?"

"You collapsed, my friend. Luckily, I managed to catch you. If you had been another minute I was going to run back and call for an ambulance. As it is, looking at the blood on your shoulder, I guess you weren't released from the hospital?"

Luke sat up and put a hand on his shoulder. It came away covered in blood but the pain was less than he expected.

"My wound was not too bad. I was only in for observation... I guess you can observe?" He didn't mention the blood loss and the possible concussion, why complicate things?

Luke looked at him for a few moments and Mason wondered if he was going to go back for that ambulance after all.

"We don't have time, Jenny doesn't have time."

Luke nodded and knelt down beside him.

"Take off your shirt," he said as he pulled a handkerchief from his pocket and then his belt from around his waist.

Mason did as he was told and hoped the wound did not look too bad. It was still bandaged; however, the bandage was soaked with blood.

Luke took his handkerchief and bundled it into a ball before pressing it hard into the wound.

Mason breathed in. "Sheeesh," he whistled through his teeth.

"It's gonna hurt more when I strap it up," Luke said as he wrapped his belt around the shoulder and over the handkerchief. "Are you ready?"

Mason nodded. He was as ready as he would ever be and he wanted the man to hurry.

Luke pulled the belt tight and, ignoring the cursing that streamed from Mason, he pulled even tighter. Then he wrapped it around and around again then pulled it tight and fastened it.

"That should stop the bleeding for now. But no more digging for you, you can sit and watch but that's it for now."

Mason nodded and watched as the priest began to dig once more.

"How did you learn how to do that?" Mason asked.

"I did a couple of years in Africa, I saw a lot worse than that... I think I found something."

Mason looked down into the hole in the ground and felt a sudden sadness. This was the grave of a child. He couldn't believe how any parent could do something quite so inhuman. Yet here they were, digging her up once more with the intent of driving her from this realm.

"Is it her?"

Luke scraped a shovel across the wood.

"I think so."

"We have to hurry," Mason said. "Don't ask me why but I just feel we have to hurry."

Luke nodded.

Mason closed his eyes tight and sent out a thought to Jenny. Stay strong, my love, I'm coming for you, just stay strong.

Chapter Twenty-Six

The tea was nearly finished and Jenny felt nervous once more. There was a look in Victoria's eyes and a sneer on her face. Something was about to happen.

The blonde girl took a long sip of pretend tea, closed her eyes and sighed in contentment. Jenny giggled and did the same.

"Oh, this tea is so good." Jenny put down her cup and then wished she hadn't.

Victoria's eyebrows rose and she put down her own cup. There was something smug about her gaze.

"You were right, it is time," Victoria said and from behind her back she pulled out a rope.

Jenny felt a lump in her throat as she recognized it as the noose. How could she get out of this?

"I don't want to play this game, why don't we play cards? We can play snap, I don't mind if you win."

"The cards are in the kitchen," Victoria said. "We can play them soon but as we are going down we may as well get this over with." She shook the noose in front of Jenny.

Jenny wanted to say no, she wanted to get up and run from that place and yet she felt strangely lethargic. She could hear Victoria talking but the words were like the wind. They whispered in her ear, they lulled her and she felt herself giving in to them. Fatigue was like a soft, warm blanket. It weighed her down and drew her in and she wanted to say yes. She couldn't remember what it was she would be saying yes to, but as Victoria spoke she wanted to agree with her. Wanted to go with her and do as she was told.

Suddenly, she thought of Mason. It was almost as if she could hear him telling her to be strong and it was like a slap to her face. It brought her back to her senses and she was afraid. The rope was in her hands and she knew she had been ready to slip it over her head. How could she have given into this child? How could she have forgotten her own family and that they needed her? Somehow, she knew that Mason was out there and that he was working to save her. All she had to do was give him a little more time but how could she do that?

Victoria was looking angry again and the pressure in the room was growing. Jenny found it hard to breathe and she knew she had to slow things down. But she had to take control, she had to be careful, Victoria must never know. Somehow, she had to stop herself from falling under the spirit's influence once more but how could she do it? Would pain help? Thinking that maybe it would, she screwed up her left fist digging her long nails into her palm until she could feel blood. It hurt but it also made her feel a little more awake. It was not much but it would have to do for now.

Victoria was holding the rope out before her and expecting her to what... to jump from the balcony? That was something she would never do, at least not if she had the choice.

Plastering a smile on her face she looked up at Victoria.

"I want to know your story first." She pouted a little. "You promised you would tell me and I want to know what happened."

The pressure increased in the room and the temperature dropped to below freezing. Even though it was dark her eyes had grown accustomed and she could see quite well. Certainly well enough to see the anger that had pinked the spirits cheeks.

"I will tell you all about my life and how

I got here," Jenny said. "After all, if we are going to be friends forever, it's only fair that we take a bit of time to understand first."

That seemed to have worked and Victoria's smile returned. It was easier to breathe and the room warmed, even if just a little bit.

"I will show you, but then it's time."

Jenny nodded and could see that Victoria was holding out her hand. Somehow, the thought of taking it filled her with dread. Yet the alternative was the rope. She could feel the coarse hemp across her lap and holding the child's hand had to be better than that... didn't it?

***

Luke kept digging until he had fully uncovered the wooden box. It looked so small, so pitifully small and he hesitated as his hand reached down to touch it. Mason came to his side and touched his shoulder.

"You want me to do it?" Mason asked.

The priest shook his head and reached down. Using the spade he levered it into the side of the box and applied some pressure. The wood and nails cracked alarmingly in the still woodland but the lid lifted a little. Pulling the spade out he moved it further down and did the same thing. Once more the crack ricocheted around the clearing.

Mason swallowed, what would they find inside the box?

Luke looked at him quickly and then moved the spade down to the bottom end and this time, as he pried the board, the lid sprang free. It lifted slightly and then dropped back into place.

Luke threw the spade aside and crossed himself before reaching down to remove the lid.

Inside the box was bare wood. Small, yellowed, old bones lay in the shape of a child. It was a sad and pitiful sight and Mason felt his breath catch. He could see the skull, the empty eyes accused him and he had to look away. Letting his gaze drift down the skeleton, he noticed the nightdress. There were only tatters of it left and yet he could recognize it. Complete with splatters of blood it was the one that Victoria was wearing the last time he had seen her.

"This is her," he said. "Now what do we do?"

Mason was worried. They had taken so long and from what he could gather, Jenny had left the hospital before midnight. That meant she had been alone with the spirit for getting on for 12 hours. How much longer would she survive?

"I have a grave prepared back in the churchyard," Luke said. "If we can get this coffin out, back to your house, and then transport it from there, this will soon be over."

"Do you think it will hold?" Mason asked as he eyed the wood suspiciously.

Luke shrugged his shoulders. It had been down here a long while and was unlikely to survive the journey. Already in places it was crumbling away to nothing. The thought of lifting it out and the little girl's bones scattering back into the grave was too much to bear.

Only Luke had come prepared. From his pocket he pulled out an old sheet. Quickly, he unfolded it and laid it on the ground. Then he knelt beside it, crossed himself once more, and blessed the sheet.

"Let's lift her onto this and transport her that way," he said.

Luke was in the hole and passed the bones up. Mason wanted to rush him. He was treating the body with reverence and respect but it was taking too long. He understood what the priest was doing but their priority should be to the living and every moment they took, Jenny was in more danger. Even so, when he felt the first bone in his hands he almost dropped it.

Luke had passed him an ulna. It was smooth and light and cold in his fingers. His first instinct was to drop it and yet he could see the priest watching him, judging him. So he slowly lowered it down to the sheet and then leaned forward for another one. They carried on this slow process for the next 20 or 30 minutes. With each bone, Mason felt a sense of dread and weakness. It was as if moving the body was draining him of his life and yet he knew that was silly, that it was foolish.

Most of the bones were moved now and the last one was the skull. All the time they had been doing this the empty, cold eyes had been watching him and they seemed to hold his gaze as the priest passed the bone up.

Mason swallowed and rubbed his sweaty palms on his jeans before he could reach out and take the skull. It felt slippery in his hands and for one awful moment he thought he would drop it. Taking a breath, he lowered it gently onto the sheet and then folded the edges of the material over to cover the bones. Only then did he feel like he could relax. As if at last they were getting somewhere.

Reaching out, he offered Mason a hand

and helped pull him from the small grave. The priest knelt before the bones and whispered a prayer.

"We have to go," Mason said. "Jenny is in danger, we have to go!"

Luke nodded and stood, grabbing hold of the sheet, he made sure that all the ends were together and then he lifted up the bones. They rattled like dry old logs and Mason felt his stomach turn.

"Lead the way."

Together they walked out of the woodland as quick as they could. Mason just hoped that they would be in time.

***

Jenny took hold of the child's cold and insubstantial hands. Instantly she took them, she felt weak and as if she was drifting. It was as if Victoria was pulling her in, pulling her away from the world and into the darkness. Quickly, she bit down on her lip, drawing blood until the pain leveled her once more.

The hands she held were firmer now. It was as if her very life was powering the spirit's body.

They were so close that they were eye to

eye and Jenny found it hard to look into the cold gray orbs before her. They reminded her of the gravestone, the one in the woods. They reminded her of death. There was nothing behind them, nothing there but an abyss so big it could suck her in and she would be lost forever.

Victoria squeezed harder and suddenly the room was gone. She was back in Abby's room, only it was different. The walls were lined with shelves and on them were row after row of old dolls. Their sightless eyes all stared into the room and it was very creepy. It was dark in the room and yet somehow she could see. From somewhere, she could hear shouting and she was afraid.

Closing her eyes, she hugged Mr. Good Bear to her chest. He was her favorite. A recent present from her mummy and he was a brave bear. Mummy told her he would always keep her safe and so far he always had. Jenny knew the thoughts were not her own, she was living what Victoria thought and she tried to talk to her. Nothing happened.

Outside it was raining and the candle had gone out long ago, leaving the room dark, cold, and scary. Lightning flashed across the sky and she jumped off the bed onto the floor and scrambled beneath it. It was safe under here, it was somewhere where the monster wouldn't find her.

Jenny understood she was living Victoria's last night and she tried to keep herself separate from the child, tried to watch it and not become fully immersed. If she did she wondered if she would be able to pull back or if Victoria would tell her to jump from the balcony and she would do as she was told.

She could feel the child's terror, feel her shivering and each time her father shouted she would squeal with dread and crawl further under the bed. Until now, there was nowhere else to go because her feet were against the wall and still the sound reached them.

Victoria thought the monster was coming. Jenny couldn't work out what the monster was. It could be a figment of her imagination, it could have been her father, but from what she had seen over the last few weeks it could be anything.

Victoria was whispering over and over again. "Safe," she whispered. "Safe in my bubble." Tears escaped her eyes and slipped down her face to land on Mr. Good Bear. "Keep quiet, must keep quiet."

Now she was talking to the bear. Jenny saw it and felt it as if she was inside the child.

"Would you help me hide Mummy?" she asked, and automatically she tilted the bear to nod his approval. It made her feel better. She was not alone.

Victoria got out from under the bed and started to walk down the corridor. Jenny was with her, seeing through her eyes and yet she wanted her to stop. Inside, she was screaming, telling Victoria not to go, to stay in her room and to hide. Yet, no matter what she said, no matter how much she shouted, Victoria kept going, now she was running. On and on down the corridor towards the monster.

Soon they were stood outside the master bedroom. The room that had always felt wrong to Jenny and now she would find out why.

As they went into the room she saw her mummy lying on the floor in front of the bed. Right where the stain was, right where it would never leave. Jenny wanted to turn and run, she tried to turn but she could not move.

Blood and bruises covered the woman's face and there was terror in her eyes. Jenny clutched Mr. Good Bear, holding him to her chest, she sucked on his ear. Normally, this would calm her but not tonight. Tears were streaming down her face and she wanted to go to Mummy's side but she could not move because the monster had gotten around her and was blocking her way. It was bigger than she remembered and twice as scary. Once more, the monster roared and Victoria wanted to cover her ears and dive beneath Mummy's bed but she could not get to it. She tried to point, tried to talk, to tell Mummy to get under the bed but no words came out and Mummy just sat there. Didn't she realize it was safe under the bed?

Lightning flooded the room and the monster turned to Victoria and suddenly it all made sense.

The monster was Daddy and he was going to eat her.

Light glinted off a blade in his right hand and then the room was plunged into darkness once more. Victoria could hear moving but she could not see anything. Standing as still as she could she tried to make herself small. That was another way to beat the monster. If you were so small, quiet, and so still it wouldn't see you. Maybe it would go right on past you.

Jenny stood in the dark, trying to be small and insignificant as she listened to Victoria's mummy sobbing.

It was unreal, she could feel the child's fear as if it was her own and yet she had no control over her limbs. The thoughts in her head were Victoria's. She was scared of the daddy monster. Jenny understood and knew what was going to happen. The man roared with hate and lightning lit up the room.

Victoria let out a scream as she saw the monster stalking closer to her mummy. A knife was raised in his hand and just before the darkness fell it slashed down. Victoria screamed and Jenny felt something warm and wet splash across her face and arms. It covered Mr. Good Bear and that made her want to cry.

She had been right all along, the stain on the bear was blood.

As her eyes became accustomed to the dark she saw the man turn towards her. Jenny tried to steer the child away, tried to make her run but instead, she felt warm liquid running down her legs and knew that Victoria had wet herself. She wept for the child but she wanted this to stop now and managed to say it.

"Stop this, you don't have to live through this again."

The vision was gone and she was back in the room.

"Have you seen enough?" Victoria asked.

Jenny nodded. She wanted to pull Victoria to her and hug her. How could any parent do this, how could the poor child have gone through such terrors? Of course, she had done so by losing her mind. That was why she became a spirit and that was why she wouldn't leave.

"Let me hold you," Jenny said and she opened her arms.

Victoria's cheeks flushed red and the room chilled. "Not until you are dead. Come with me now!"

Jenny wanted to resist but she felt cold and weak and for some reason, as Victoria offered her the noose, she put it around her neck. It was heavy and she wanted to lie down and sleep and yet Victoria was going. She faded through the walls and Jenny knew she must follow her. It was important, it was to save someone, she just couldn't remember who. So she dropped down onto the floor and crawled out of the little room and into the attic with the rope dragging behind her. Soon this would be over and then she could rest.

Chapter Twenty-Seven

They had made it out of the woodland and piled the sheet with the bones into the back of Luke's aging Ford Mondeo. Quickly, they climbed into the car and Mason looked up at the house. It seemed so peaceful, so quaint and yet he knew that inside it was full of terrors.

"We have to hurry," Mason said.

Luke was fiddling with the ignition key, he nodded and turned it. The car turned over lazily but did not fire. The priest pumped the accelerator pedal a few times and tried again. This time there was nothing.

Mason wanted to scream, instead, he clenched his fists and prayed the next time it would work. Once more the priest turned the ignition and this time the engine fired and roared into life.

Soon they were driving along the small and twisty roads going much too slow for

Mason's liking.

"My wife is with that... spirit, ghost, child, whatever it is, she has my wife and she is in danger."

Luke pushed the accelerator a little bit faster and the car sped forward. Still, the journey seemed to take forever and Mason wished he had stayed at the house. There was nothing he could do now, nothing he could help with here and if he had stayed maybe he could have saved Jenny. For the longer it took them, the further he went from the house, the more he believed that his wife was already dead.

At last, they pulled up into the churchyard and Luke stopped the car before an open grave. They both got out and went to the back seat to grab the sheet. Before they lifted it, Luke stopped.

"We need salt," he said. "Wait here, while I fetch some, but don't do anything."

Mason nodded and he looked at his watch, it was almost one o'clock. What had taken so much time?

***

Jenny followed Victoria down the two sets of stairs and to the main hallway. Dread filled her as they walked past the master bedroom but the door was closed and nothing happened. Soon, they were on the balcony at the corner of the hallway. It was directly above the stain on the carpet and she knew what would happen.

Desperately, she tried to stop. To dig in her heels and at least slow down but it was as if she was being pulled by Victoria and she must just follow on wherever she led. Stood leaning over the balcony was the monster. She shook her head as he was just a man. A bad father and husband and he meant her harm but just a man, nevertheless. Dark brows were scrunched down and a long nose made him look mean and evil. Jenny wondered if he ever smiled, for his face did not seem capable of it.

She tried to clench her fists. To dig her nails into her palms but her hands wouldn't obey as she watched the man grab hold of Victoria.

It was not this Victoria but one from long ago. She does not know if the man was here or if this was a vision that Victoria wanted her to see. The older version of the child was terrified, as was the younger. Her red face all scrunched up and she was crying and trying to get away. Only, she was weak and so afraid that she thought it better to stand still. That was so like a child that Jenny felt her heart break. How could this happen?

As she watched, the man tied the rope to the banister and put the noose around the child's neck. Then he lifted her.

"No," Jenny screamed but he could not hear her for he was not there. This was just a memory.

For a moment, Victoria turned and her desperate eyes seemed to find Jenny. They cried out for help, for justice, for anything to stop the horror that was happening. Only the man didn't care. Rage was coming off him in waves and like a physical force. Once the noose was around her neck he lifted her onto the banister rail. The child whimpered and squeezed her eyes tightly shut. In a desperate effort her hands clasped onto her father's shirt. She was so afraid she would not let go. Anger clouded his face and he grasped her fingers so roughly that Jenny heard one break as he peeled them from him.

She let out a gasp and her own hands could move. It was as if she felt the pain of the break in her own fingers and for a moment she had control. Instead of moving back she rushed forward. Maybe she could save the child.

As she watched him peel finger after finger from his shirt she was getting closer. Reaching out now, maybe she could clasp onto the child's nightdress? Maybe she could save her. Only it was too late. As she watched, he grinned at his daughter.

With big gray eyes filled with tears she looked up at him and her final words were brave, "You will pay for this," she whispered in a voice that was barely a breeze. "All who ignore me will pay."

As Jenny reached out as far as she could he pushed Victoria from the railing and Jenny's fingers touched only empty space.

Like an angel, the child fell out into the blackness. Soaring down so beautifully until the rope snapped her to a stop and the sound of her neck breaking was like a gunshot in the quiet house.

"Now, it is your turn," Victoria said. "Then we can be together, forever."

Jenny felt herself moving towards the banister rail. She had every intention of climbing over and jumping into the abyss and yet she didn't know why. Tears were streaming down her face and she wanted to help this child. If being with her would do that then was it too much to ask?

Slowly, she stepped up to the banister. There was a chair next to it and she was ready to climb up and take that final step.

***

Mason paced by the tiny grave. What was taking so long? He was doing his best to not look at the grave or the bones. Everything seemed so small and each time he did he felt tears prickle at the back of his eyes. Though he was desperate to have this finished and to get back to the house and check on Jenny, seeing the grave had affected him deeply. There was a small and rather plain wooden box in the grave. It had a cross on the lid but had obviously been put together quickly and was not quite what he expected of a coffin. For a moment he thought of Abby and worried about her being left alone in the hospital. Would she be scared? How would a parent ever cope with the loss of a child? He did not think he could, just the thought was enough to break him.

Luke was coming back towards him and the sight of the priest running across the grass was enough to lift his head. In his hands he carried a big pot of salt and a Bible. Breathlessly, he arrived at the side of the grave.

"I need to do this," Luke said. "To make sure I will pray and lay her to rest. Please, be patient just a few moments longer."

Mason shook his head and yet inside he was screaming hurry!

Luke went to the grave and lifted the lid of the little coffin. It was lined with sheets and a small pillow. Then he came to the car and took out the bones. All the time he was praying but it was in Latin and Mason could not understand.

Gently, he laid the sheet in the coffin and then he opened it up. As he did the wind whipped around the trees in the churchyard and they both looked up.

Was it the child? Was she fighting this?

As they shared a glance, the wind fell and Mason let out a breath. Hopefully, that was natural and Jenny was keeping the spirit busy.

"Stay strong, my love," he whispered. "We are coming for you, just stay strong."

Looking back at the grave he could see the priest had arranged the bones in a rough order.

"Hurry!" he called.

Luke nodded and sprinkled salt over the bones. Nothing happened. Mason was not sure what he expected but he had expected something. Despair came over him and he looked at Luke.

"Is it over?"

"No, I have to pray, just be patient."

Mason nodded but patience had never been his strong point.

"Blessed are those who have died in the Lord; let them rest from their labors for their good deeds go with them."

***

Jenny felt the rope dragging as she climbed up onto the chair. It was just a step up now and she could fall and be with her friend forever more. She was excited and yet, something nagged at the back of her mind. There was something wrong. Something waiting for her but she couldn't quite remember what it was. As she looked over she felt herself giggle and the sound shocked her. She sounded older than she expected. Wasn't she young?

"You have to jump now," Victoria said and reached out a hand to push her.

Jenny looked down and remembered Victoria flying through the air. It had looked such fun and she wanted to try it. It was as if she was compelled to do as she was told and yet there was something telling her not to. Every now and then she saw a young girl's face. She had pretty black hair and a sweet smile. She wanted to play with her and yet she was tired. If she fell then she would be able to rest and maybe they could play with the dolls again.

"Can we play with the dolls?" Jenny asked as she got off the chair.

Victoria was angry. She knew because it always went cold when she was angry. Then her cheeks pinched and her lips thinned to almost a line. The last thing she wanted was to make her friend angry but why did she have to play this game? She was tired.

"You have to jump first," Victoria said, and she grabbed Jenny's arm. Her fingers were like ice and they dug painfully into Jenny's skin. Then she pushed and pulled Jenny until she was back on the chair.

"You have to jump so that we can be a family, you, me and the baby."

"Baby?" Jenny asked. There were so many questions back in her mind. Baby? Family? Didn't she already have a family? Then she remembered the name, Abby. Her beautiful daughter, Abby. If she jumped she would be leaving her, leaving Mason and the baby! Was that why she had felt so sick, why she craved ice cream? There was no way she could do this. No way she could jump.

"We can have parties and be together, forever. We will make it so no one wants to live here and we can be all alone," Victoria said as she tried to shove her towards the balcony.

As she touched her, Jenny felt her mind wandering and she wanted to do as she was told. Quickly, she clenched her fists and dug her nails into her hands. The sharp pain brought her back and she saw where she was. Fear made her gasp and she felt her arms prickle with adrenaline. What was she doing?

"No," Jenny shouted. "No, I won't do this."

She tried to step off the chair but rage hit her hard and she was pushed towards the edge. The ice cold spirit was like a whirlwind as she pushed and pulled and tugged Jenny towards the void. The noose tightened on her neck and she felt herself slip. The chasm below was like a great yawning hole and she tried to pull back. Hands grabbed her as her own tried to release the noose and fight off the attack. Soon, she did not know which way was which and panic filled her as fear clawed at her chest.

"Keep calm," the sound steadied her a little. "I am not afraid. You are not welcome here!" she shouted the words but she was getting weaker and the urge to take that step was strong. "No. No, never!"

***

Luke continued to pray and sprinkled holy water over the bones, followed by another layer of salt.

Mason was watching him, waiting for something to happen, anything to show them that this had worked. There was a feeling of desperation inside him. A feeling of failure and despair and yet he must not give in. So, he closed his eyes and tried to send help to Jenny.

"I love you so much. Fight her, fight her for Abby and for me. Fight her for life and because it is right."

The wind picked up and the trees around them were suddenly waving and tossing as a gust of air raced down the driveway and up to the grave. Mason had to spread his legs to keep his ground and he watched Luke as he too was knocked about. The wind was dark, like a shadow, and Mason felt a lump form in his throat. Was this it? Was she here?

Luke was almost blown over but he steadied himself and continued to pray. His hand was on his Bible. "O Lord, grant eternal rest unto this poor soul. Let Your perpetual light shine upon Victoria Pennyford. May the soul of the faithfully departed, through the mercy of God, rest in peace. Amen." Luke closed the Bible and looked up as if to challenge the very wind itself.

The shadow formed and circled him, buffeting him and yet he would not move. Then it swarmed down and into the coffin. Once it was all inside there was peace once more and the lid of the small and insubstantial coffin slammed shut.

Mason let out a gasp of air. "Is it over?"

"I think so." Luke stepped towards the grave and threw a single pink carnation onto the coffin.

Mason had not seen the flower before but thought that the priest must have prepared even this beautiful gesture. Now he wanted to go. To find Jenny, and yet his car was back at the house and he could see that Luke wanted to see that the grave was filled. With difficulty, he stood and looked as solemn as he could.

"Here." Luke passed over his keys. "Take my car and I pray that Jenny is safe."

Mason nodded. "Thanks."

"We did a good thing here," Luke said as Mason ran for the car.

Mason gunned the car and reversed down the narrow driveway as fast as he could. He knew the priest was right. That is was good to put the child to rest. It would prevent her hurting others but it was also the best thing for her. She was so tormented and this was a great release and yet all he could see was Jenny's sweet face. Though his shoulder hurt and a wave of dizziness engulfed him, he pushed the car faster along the narrow and twisty lanes. What would he do if they were too late? Would they have to do the same ritual for Jenny?

That thought was too hard to even contemplate.

***

Jenny was losing the fight. Victoria was stronger than she was and each time she touched her it was sapping her will to fight and yet she had to. Abby and Mason needed her and if she was pregnant... then she owed it to the child. It made sense, the sickness and the sudden craving for ice-cream. It was something she never liked and yet the first time she was pregnant it was all she wanted to eat.

The room was so cold and Victoria had a hold on her arm. She was dragging her towards the balcony. Pushing and pulling and Jenny wanted to give in, she wanted to let go. Her only weapon seemed to be the pain and yet if she dug her nails into her hands she couldn't fight back. Couldn't hold onto the banister and try and stop the fall. In the end, she released her fingers and instantly she felt herself relax and give into the spirit. It was like a wave of fatigue washed over her and carried her along with it. How could she stop the feeling? She was no longer resisting, no longer digging in her heels, and though she wanted to remove the noose, she could not force her hands to move. Then she thought of Abby and she bit down on her lip. This time she kept biting until blood ran into her mouth and tears streamed out of her eyes. It gave her back a sense of will but it also incensed Victoria.

"You have to come with me," she screamed and suddenly there was a whirlwind in the house. The pressure from the wind swept Jenny ever closer to the banister. She could feel it lift her from her feet and she knew it was too late.

"No," she screamed and she grabbed the noose and pulled it from her neck. If she fell it may still kill her or paralyze her but it would not be a hanging. She would not go the way the spirit wanted. The wind swept her up over the railing but she clung on for dear life. Though her arms screamed in pain and her shoulders were almost wrenched from the socket she hung on.

"You are not welcome here," she shouted through clenched teeth. "Go!"

As if on her command the wind dropped and she was left hanging by her arms. The house was deadly silent and felt peaceful in a way she had never known. Everything came back to her. Who she was, her family, and how close she had come. Sobbing, she tried to pull herself up but it was no good. Her weight was too much and her arms could hardly support her. Then she heard a car pulling up and she looked to the door. It was Luke's car.

"In here," she shouted. "Help me."

The pain was so much that she wondered if she could hold on but she heard footsteps running up the stairs. Her eyes were closed now as she clung on for grim death, but then she felt a hand touch hers and she looked up into Mason's face.

Quickly he grasped onto her arm and hauled her over the banister. They both collapsed onto the floor and she rested her head on his shoulder.

"How you doing?" he asked, panting between each word.

"Good," she managed. "You?"

Mason laughed and pulled her to him and kissed her head.

"I'm good too, but I think I pulled my stitches."

"Typical of a man, can never rest when he's told to." Jenny turned and checked his arm. He was right. "It looks like another visit to the hospital. What should we tell them?"

Mason doubled over laughing. "I suggest a break in," he managed when he finally controlled himself.

Jenny nodded.

Epilogue

One Year Later.

Jenny walked around the garden and through the artists who were enjoying her latest retreat. It was a year to the day of them laying Victoria to rest and later they were celebrating.

Gail Parker and her boyfriend, Jesse, were coming for a meal with them and Luke, the priest, would be there also. They had so much to be grateful for and so much to thank these people for and yet she knew that it would not be mentioned.

Gail and Jesse had arrived the morning following all the excitement. They were very disappointed to have missed everything but eager to learn all they could. Since then they had become good friends. Mason even helped them with their website and accounts from time to time. They had come into the house and checked everything over and had assured them that all was fine. It seemed so strange to see them walking around with their meters and cameras, almost like a television show. Once they had been through the house twice they assured them that Victoria was gone. Still, Jenny managed to persuade them to stay for a few nights and she felt so much better after that.

There had been no more occurrences, nothing at all. They had even managed to clean the stains from the carpets and this time they never returned.

Abby seemed to remember nothing and yet she no longer wanted to sleep in her old room. Mason quickly decorated one of the guest suites in a bright and sunny yellow and she moved next to their room. It felt much better and much safer when the guests arrived. They even had a door fitted so that their part of the house was private.

Jenny had cleaned out the attic and now used it as a storeroom. It seemed such a sad little place but once again, with some good lighting and a coat of white paint, it was a different place.

Jenny stopped behind one of her artists.

"Slow down, Mark," she said. "It's not a race and you are not allowing your senses to appreciate what is before you. Once you do, you will be able to transfer that feeling to the canvas. It's not just about what you see... it's mostly about how you feel."

Mark nodded a head covered in shaggy ginger hair and looked a little bashful.

Jenny moved on. Life was so good. She got time to paint and to explain her methods to other artists. Her retreats were getting excellent reviews and she was now booked up two years in advance. Mason was working from home and had just a dozen clients. That gave him time to help her and to help look after the guests.

Over to one side, Abby was sat with her brother, James. He was the sweetest child with jet black hair and pale blue eyes. Jenny would not call them gray. Not after what had happened, but she had to admit that at times they bore a resemblance to Victoria's. There was something else that disturbed her. Mason told her it was ridiculous and yet she could not shake a feeling of dread. The stain. The one in the hallway had been in the shape of an angel. After she had seen Victoria fall she understood, but Mason had never seen it. Could never understand how she saw the shape, but she could. Now her son had a birthmark on his right shoulder in the exact same shape.

Was he her little angel or was the mark something more foreboding? Jenny knew that it could be nothing, could be just a coincidence, or her stressed mind looking for trouble and yet sometimes when she saw it she felt the room chill.

***

THE END

Never miss a book.

Subscribe to Caroline Clark's newsletter

for new release announcements

and occasional free content:

http://eepurl.com/cGdNvX

Preview: The Haunting of Brynlee House

25th April 15 82
The basement of the cage.
Derbyshire.
England.

3:15 am.

Alden Carter looked down at his shaking hands. The sight of blood curdled his stomach as it dripped onto the floor. For a moment, his resolve failed, he did not recognize the thin, gnarled fingers. Did not recognize the person he had become. How could he do this, how could he treat another human being in this terrible way and yet he knew he must. If he did not, then the consequences for him would be grave. For a second he imagined a young girl with a thin face and a long nose. Her brown hair bounced as she ran in circles and she flashed a smile each time she passed. The memory brought him joy and comfort. Brook was not a pretty girl, but she was his daughter, and he loved her more than he could say. He remembered her joy at the silver cross he gave her. The one that he was given from the Bishop, the one that cost him his soul.

Rubbing his hands through sparse hair, he almost gagged at the feeling of the crusty blood he found there. How many times had he run those blood-soaked fingers through his lank and greasy hair? Too many to count. It had been a long night, and it was not over yet. This must be done, and it was him who had to do it.

Suddenly, his throat was dry, and fatigue weighed him down like the black specter of death he had become. A candle flickered and cast a grotesque shadow across the wall. Outside, the trees shook their skeletal fingers against the brick and wood house and he closed his eyes for a moment. Seeing Brook once more he strengthened his resolve. The trees trembled, and the wind seemed to whisper through their leaves, tormenting him, telling him that he was wrong but he would not stop. Could not stop.

Taking a breath, he felt stronger now, and with a shaky hand, he picked up an old stein and took a drink of bitter ale. It did not quench his thirst, but it gave him a little courage. He must do this. He must go back down to the cage and finish what he had started, for if he did not Brook would not survive and maybe neither would he?

The kitchen was sparse and dark and yet he knew he was lucky. The house was made of brick as well as wood. It was three stories' high and was bigger than he needed. This was a luxury few could afford. As was the plentiful supply of food in the pantry and work every day. The Bishop had been kind to him, and he knew he had much to be grateful for. Yet, what price had he paid? As the wind picked up, the trees got angry and seemed to curse him with their branches. Rattling against the walls and making ghostly shadows through the window.

Alden turned from them and up to the wall before him. The sight of it almost stopped his heart and yet he knows he must go back down to the cage. If the Bishop found him up here with his job not done, then he would be in trouble... Brook would be in trouble. A shiver ran down his spine as he approached the secret door. Reaching out a shaky hand he touched the wall. It was cold, hard and yet it gave before him. With a push, the catch released and the door swung inward. Before him was a dark empty space. A chasm, an evil pit that he must descend into once more.

Picking up the oil lamp, he approached the stairs and slowly walked down into the dark. The walls were covered in whitewash, and yet they did not seem light. Nothing about this place seemed light. Shadows chased across the ceiling behind him and then raced in front as if eager to reach the hell below. Cobwebs clawed at his face. These did not bother Alden, he did not fear the spider, no, it was the serpent in God's clothing who terrified him.

With each step, the temperature dropped. He had never understood why it was so much colder down here. Cellars were always cool, but this one... with each step, he felt as if he was falling into the lake. That he had broken through the ice and was sinking into the water. Panic clenched his stomach as he wondered if he would drown. The air seemed to stagnate in his lungs, and they ached as he tried to pull in a breath. It was just panic, he shook it off, and was back on the stairs. His feet firm on the stone steps he descended deeper and deeper. He shrugged into his thick, coarse jacket. The material would not protect him, of that he was sure, but he pushed such thoughts to the back of his mind and stepped onto the soft soil of the basement floor.

There was an old wooden table to his right. Quickly, he put the oil lamp on it. Shadows chased across the room. In front of him, his work area was just touched with the light, he knew he must look confident as he approached the woman shackled to the wall. Ursula Kemp was once a beauty. With red hair and deep green eyes. Her smooth ivory skin was traced with freckles, and she had always worn a smile that had the local men bowing to her every need. Seven years ago she had married the blacksmith, and they had a daughter, Rose. Alden felt his eyes pulled to his right... there in the shadows lay a pile of bones.

A small pile, the empty eyes of the skull accused him. Though he could not look away from that blackened, burned, mound... the cause of another stain on his soul. Bile rose in his throat, and the air seemed full of smoke. It was just his imagination, he swallowed, choked down a cough and pulled his eyes away. Blinking back tears, he turned and looked up at Ursula. Chained to the wall she should be beaten, broken, and yet there was defiance in her eyes. They were like a cool stream on a hot summer's day. Something about them defied the position she was in. How could she not be beaten? How could she not confess?

"Confess witch," he said the words with more force than he felt. Fear and anger fired his speech and maybe just a little shame. "Confess, and this will be over."

Ursula's eyes stared back at him cool,

calm, unmoving. She looked across at the bones, and he expected her to break. Yet her face was calm... her lips twitched into a smile.

Alden's eyes followed hers. The bones were barely visible in the dark, but he could still see them as clear as day. A glint of something sparkled in the lamplight, but he did not see it. All he could see was the bones. Sweat formed on his palms as if his hands remembered putting them there. Remembered how they felt, strangely smooth and powdery beneath his fingers. *Ash is like silk on the fingers...* a sob almost escaped him, and for a second he wanted to free Ursula, to tell her to run... and yet, if he did then the Bishop may turn him and Brook into a heap of ash like the one he was trying to not look at.

In his mind, he heard the sound of a screaming child, the sound of the flames. Smelt the burning, an almost tantalizing scent of roasting meat. Shaking his head, he pushed the thoughts away. Now was the time for strength. Biting down on his lip, he fought back the tears and turned to face her once more.

"You will not break me," she shouted defiantly. "Unlike you, I have done no wrong. Kill me, and I will haunt you and your family until the end of time."

Alden turned as anger overrode his judgment, striding to the table he picked up a knife. It was thin, cruel, and the blade glinted in the lamplight. Controlling the shaking of his hands, he crossed the room and plunged it into her side. For a second it caught... stopped by the thickness of her skin. Controlled by rage, he leaned all his strength against it and it sliced into her. Slick, warm blood poured across his fingers. "Confess, confess NOW," he screamed spraying her face with spittle.

A noise from above set his heart beating at such a rate that he thought she must hear it. It pounded in his chest and reminded him of his favorite horse as it galloped across the fields.

The Bishop was here.

Without a confession, he was damned, but maybe he was damned anyway. Maybe his actions doomed him to never rest, yet he must save his daughter, he must save his darling Brook.

As he heard the door above open, panic filled his mind, he must act now, or it would be too late. Then he saw it in her eyes, Ursula knew what was coming. She knew she would die soon and yet she did not fear it. Maybe she thought she would meet her daughter, that they would be together again. He did not know, but the calm serenity in her eyes chilled him to the bone.

In a fit of rage, he struck her on the temple. The light left her eyes, her head dropped forward, and she was unconscious, but it no longer mattered... he had a plan.

"You have confessed," he shouted. "You are a witch. By the power of the church, I sentence you to death, you will be hung by the neck until you die."

Before the Bishop reached him, he pulled back his hand and slapped her hard across the face. The slap did not wake her, but the noise resounded across the cellar. As the Bishop stopped behind him, he felt an even deeper chill. This man had no morals, no conscience. Alden knew what he had done was wrong, but he did not care. If it kept his family safe, he would sacrifice any number of innocents, and yet his stomach turned at the thought of what was to come.

"You have your confession," the Bishop's voice was harsh in the darkness. "Let us hang her and end this terrible business."

***

Ursula woke to the feel of rough, coarse hemp around her neck. As her eyes came open, she felt the pain in her side and knew it was a mortal wound. The agony of it masked the multiple injuries she had received over the past few days.

Alden was holding her. Hoisting her up onto a platform which was suspended over the rail of the balcony. The rope tightened as he placed her feet on the smooth wood and fear filled her. This was it, she knew what was coming, and yet she shook the fear away. To her side, the Bishop stood, a lace handkerchief in his hand as he dabbed at the powder on his face. Blond hair covered a plump but handsome visage, with good bones and a wide mouth, but his eyes... they were gray and hard. The color of a gravestone they could cut through granite with just a look. Amusement danced in them, or maybe it was just the lamp flickering. It could not provide nearly enough for her to really tell, and yet she knew.

Alden moved away from her and turned to the Bishop. There was a hardness to him too. His lips were drawn tight enough to make a thin line, but he could not fool her. Alden was afraid, and she pitied him, pitied the days to come. For her, it was over. Death would be a sweet release, but for Alden, it had only just begun. As he pushed the table, she looked down to the floor below. The lamp did not light more than half way, and it seemed that she would jump into a bottomless pit. If the rope did not stop her... then maybe she could fly. Down deep she hoped she would soar, away from pain, away from fear and safe in the knowledge she held.

If only.

The moon came from behind a cloud and shone through the window at her back. Its light cast shadows through the branches of a large, old oak tree. Sketchy fingers coalesced on the far wall, and her heart pounded in her chest.

Was this a sign?

A welcome?

The shadows danced and then formed and appeared to be a finger pointing to her doom.

It was time.

Before Alden could push her, she stepped out into nothing.

Read

The Haunting of Seafield House

Available on Amazon

Preview: The Haunting of Seafield House

30th June 1901
Seafield House.
Barton Flats,
Yorkshire.
England.

00:01 am

    Jenny Thornton sucked in a tortured breath and hunkered down behind the curtains. The coarse material seemed to stick to her face, to cling there as if holding her down. Fighting back the thought and the panic it engendered she crouched even lower and tried to stop the shaking of her knees, to still the panting of her breath. It was imperative that she did not breathe too loudly, that she kept quiet and still. If she was to survive with just a beating, then she knew she must hide. Tonight he was worse than she had ever seen him before. Somehow, tonight was different, she could feel it in the air.

Footsteps approached on the landing. They were easy to hear through the door and seemed to mock her as they approached. Each step was like another punch to her stomach, and she could feel them reverberating through her bruises. Why had she not fled the house?

As if in answer, lightening flashed across the sky and lit up the sparsely furnished room. There was nothing between her and the door. A dresser to her right provided no shelter for an adult yet her eyes were drawn to the door on its front. It did not move but stood slightly ajar. Inside, her precious Alice would keep quiet. They had played this game before, and the child knew that she must never come out when Daddy was angry. When he was shouting. Would it be enough to keep her safe? Why had Jenny chosen this room? Before she could think, thunder boomed across the sky and she let out a yelp.

Tears were running down her face, had he heard her? It seemed unlikely that he could hear such a noise over the thunder and yet the footsteps had stopped. Oh my, he was coming back. Jenny tried to make herself smaller and to shrink into the thick velvet curtains, but there was nowhere else to go.

If only she had listened to her father, if only she had told him about Alice. For a moment, all was quiet, she could hear the house creak and settle as the storm raged outside. The fire would have burned low, and soon the house would be cold. This was the least of her problems. Maybe she should leave the room and lead Abe away from their daughter. Maybe it was her best choice. Their best choice.

Lightning flashed across the sky and filled the room with shadows. Jenny let out a scream for he was already there. A face like an overstuffed turkey loomed out of the darkness, and a hand grabbed onto her dress. Jenny was hauled off her feet and thrown across the room. Her neck hit the top of the dresser, and she slumped to the floor next to the door. How she wanted to warn Alice to stay quiet, to stay inside but she could not make a sound. There was no pain, no feeling and yet she knew that she was broken. Something had snapped when she hit the cabinet, and somehow she knew it could never be fixed. That it was over for her. In her mind, she prayed that her daughter, the child who had become her daughter, would be safe just before a distended hand reached out and grabbed her around the neck. There was no feeling just a strange burning in her lungs. The fact that she did not fight seemed to make him angrier and she was picked up and thrown again.

As she hit the window, she heard the glass shatter, but she did not feel the impact.

Did not feel anything. Suddenly, the realization hit her and she wanted to scream, to wail out the injustice of it but her mouth would not move. Then he was bending over her.

"Beg for your life, woman," Abe Thornton shouted and sprayed her with spittle.

Jenny tried to open her mouth, not to beg for her own life but to beg for that of her daughter's. She wanted to ask him to tell others about the child they had always kept a secret, the one that he had denied. To admit that they had a daughter and maybe to let the child go to her grandparents. Only her mouth would not move, and no sound came from her throat.

She could see the red fury in his eyes, could feel the pressure building up inside of him and yet she could not even blink in defense. This was it, the end, and for a moment, she welcomed the release. Then she thought of Alice, alone in that cupboard for so long. Now, who would visit her, who would look after her? There was no one, and she knew she could never leave her child.

Abe grabbed her by the front of her dress and lifted her high above his head. The anger was like a living beast inside him, and he shook her like she was nothing but a rag doll. Then with a scream of rage, he threw her. This time she saw the curtains flick against her face and then there was nothing but air.

The night was dark, rain streamed down, and she fell with it. Alongside it she fell, tumbling down into the darkness. In her mind she wheeled her arms, in her mind she screamed out the injustice, but she never moved, never made a sound.

Instead, she just plummeted toward the earth.

Lightning flashed just before she hit the ground. It lit up the jagged rocks at the base of the house, lit up the fate that awaited her and then it was dark. Jenny was overwhelmed with fear and panic, but there was no time to react, even if she could. Jenny smashed into the rocks with a hard thump and then a squelch, but she did not feel a thing.

"Alice, I will come back for you," she said in her mind. Then it was dark, it was cold, and there was nothing.

Read

The Haunting of Seafield House

Available on Amazon

Never miss a book.

Subscribe to Caroline Clark's newsletter

for new release announcements

and occasional free content:

http://eepurl.com/cGdNvX

I am also a member of the haunted house collective.

Why not discover great new authors like me?

Enter your email address to get weekly newsletters of hot new haunted house books:

http://.hauntedhousebooks.info

About the Author

Caroline Clark is a British author who has always loved the macabre, the spooky, and anything that goes bump in the night.

She was brought up on stories from James Herbert, Shaun Hutson, Darcy Coates, and Ron Ripley. Even at school she was always living in her stories and was often asked to read them out in front of the class, though her teachers did not always appreciate her more sinister tales.

Now she spends her time researching haunted houses or imagining what must go on in them. These tales then get written up and become her books.

Caroline is married and lives in Yorkshire with her husband and their two white boxer dogs. Of course one of them is called **Spooky.**

You can contact Caroline via her Facebook page:

https://www.facebook.com/CarolineClarkAuthor/

She loves to hear from her readers.

SPOOKY NIGHT BOOKS

Copyright

©Copyright 2017 Caroline Clark

All Rights Reserved

License Notes

This Book is licensed for personal enjoyment only. It may not be resold or given away to others. If you wish to share this book, please purchase an additional copy. If you are reading this book and it was not purchased then, you should purchase your own copy. Your continued respect for author's rights is appreciated.

This story is a work of fiction any resemblance to people is purely coincidence. All places, names, events, businesses, etc. are used in a fictional manner.

All characters are from the imagination of the author.

Printed in Great Britain
by Amazon